Tyrone grabbed his sneakers and quickly laced them up. He and Marla crawled out of the tent, and saw Mark. He was standing at the edge of the camp, splattered with blood from head to toe. He walked forward, stiff-legged, his eyes like headlights. In one hand he held what looked like a human limb. In the other he gripped his machete, slicing it back and forth through the air.

"I got hungry, and those Indians looked good to eat," Mark growled. His voice reverberated across the campsite, unnaturally loud. He dropped the limb. It was a man's arm, hacked from the body at the shoulder. He stepped closer. The machete whistled back and forth through the chill dawn air.

Tyrone raised the ax and clenched it tightly with both hands. "Mark, throw down the machete," he warned. "I don't want to hurt you. We can get you help, you have to believe that!"

Mark laughed, but it sounded forced. "I don't need help, Tyrone. I need to eat!"

Mark lunged at Tyrone like a wild animal, bringing the machete down at his head.

"Stop it!" Marla shrieked.

Don't miss these other Bantam Starfire Horror titles:

KILL THE TEACHER'S PET by Joseph Locke
PETRIFIED by Joseph Locke
KISS OF DEATH by Joseph Locke
GAME OVER by Joseph Locke
THE KILLING BOY by Gloria Miklowitz
DESPERATE PURSUIT by Gloria Miklowitz
FIRE MASK by Charles Grant

THE SCARED TO DEATH TRILOGY:

BOBBY'S WATCHING
BOBBY'S BACK
BRIDESMAIDS IN BLACK

THE MIDNIGHT PLACE SERIES:

DAUGHTER OF DARKNESS
SOMETHING'S WATCHING
DEATH CYCLE
HE TOLD ME TO

CALL OF THE WENDIGO

ROBIN HARDY

BANTAM BOOKS
NEW YORK • TORONTO • LONDON • SYDNEY • AUCKLAND

RL 5.5, age 012 and up

CALL OF THE WENDIGO

A Bantam Book / January 1994

The Starfire logo is a registered trademark of Bantam Books, a division of Bantam Doubleday Dell Publishing Group, Inc. Registered in U.S. Patent and Trademark Office and elsewhere.

"The Wendigo" from *Verses from 1929 On* by Ogden Nash is reprinted by permission of Little, Brown and Company and Curtis Brown Limited. Copyright © 1953 by Ogden Nash.

All rights reserved.
Text copyright © 1994 by Robin Hardy
Cover art copyright © 1994 by Larry Elmore
No part of this book may be reproduced or transmitted in any form or by any means, electronic or mechanical, including photocopying, recording, or by any information storage and retrieval system, without permission in writing from the publisher. For information address: Bantam Doubleday Dell Books for Young Readers.

If you purchased this book without a cover you should be aware that this book is stolen property. It was reported as "unsold and destroyed" to the publisher and neither the author nor the publisher has received any payment for this "stripped book."

ISBN 0-553-29828-3

Published simultaneously in the United States and Canada

Bantam Books are published by Bantam Books, a division of Bantam Doubleday Dell Publishing Group, Inc. Its trademark, consisting of the words "Bantam Books" and the portrayal of a rooster, is Registered in U.S. Patent and Trademark Office and in other countries. Marca Registrada. Bantam Books, 1540 Broadway, New York, New York 10036.

PRINTED IN THE UNITED STATES OF AMERICA

RAD 0 9 8 7 6 5 4 3 2 1

*For Nana Hardy,
Matriarch of a great northern clan,
On her ninetieth birthday*

CALL OF THE WENDIGO

CHAPTER 1

Winter blew into the city for a second time that year, on a Tuesday in early May, long after anyone expected it to get cold again. An icy arctic air mass from Canada swept across the Great Lakes, dragged toward the eastern seaboard by a sudden low pressure area above the Atlantic. An odd weather pattern for that time of year. By the time it hit New York City, TV bulletins predicted that buds would freeze, and tree branches, filled with sap, might snap under the weight of snow.

Looking back, it all made sense. That was also the first day Marla Drake realized she was being followed.

She had been at Jean-Michel's studio since just after sunrise, for a photo shoot that lasted almost eight hours. When she left the building on West 16th Street, the sky was as gray as lead, and the air felt clammy and oppressive. In the street, cars chafed in bumper-to-bumper traffic. An icy wind stirred along the sidewalk, and suddenly Marla had a pervasive, unmistakable sensation that she was being watched. Invisible eyes were boring into the back of her head.

She spun around and glanced quickly up the street to the corner. A long shadow, cast by the honky-tonk lights of a bodega, had fallen across the sidewalk. It retreated as she looked, as if whoever cast it had drawn back. Then it was gone.

Marla pulled her lapis-blue wool jacket tightly around her shoulders, and almost instinctively began to rummage in her little knapsack for the chocolate bar she knew was there. What on earth was she thinking, she asked herself, looking quickly back at the corner. It was just a shadow.

"Marla!"

She turned to see a svelte auburn-haired girl hurrying out of the building's glass doors. It was Barbara, another model who had worked on the shoot. Both of them were with Snap!, an agency that specialized in representing teen models. Barbara's "feature" was her lips, which were broad and sensuous. A Julia Roberts look-alike, everyone said. Marla was lithe, small-chested, and petite-boned with long, shiny chestnut-brown hair. A perfect Chanel six except that her head was just a little too big for her small body. At least she thought so. It made her look younger than her seventeen years.

Barbara pulled up beside her, and then, suddenly noticing the cold, looked momentarily troubled. "What happened to spring?" she complained. Without waiting for an answer, she turned back to Marla and smiled. "You busy tonight?"

"Homework," Marla said, thinking of the day at

school she'd just missed, and the work she had to catch up on, and the good grades she had to make to please her mother. She glanced at the traffic, searching for a taxi.

"You want to go on a very cool date tonight? Double date, actually," Barbara asked. She added, " 'Cept my date's not blind. I mean, it's Cubbie Cube."

"Cubbie Cube? The rap singer?" Marla knew that Barbara hung out in the music scene. This wasn't the first time she was dating a guy with a hit record.

Barbara nodded and smiled triumphantly. "We met last week backstage after his big concert at Madison Square Garden."

"And you want me along on a date with him?" Marla looked dubiously at Barbara, sure there had to be a catch.

Barbara shivered as a dervy wind swirled paper cups and rumpled newspapers in a tiny cyclone about their legs. "He's bringing a friend along." She shrugged.

Marla laughed, her resolve to stay home that night fading as the temptation to meet a wildly successful pop star grew. "And you want me to distract him so you can have Cubbie Cube to yourself."

"Will you?" Barbara brightened. "We're starting at the Universal Grill for dinner. It's down in the Village and it's the latest restaurant in New York right now." She blinked coyly, her sensuous lips spreading in a dreamy smile. "But after we eat . . . who knows?"

The Willa Cather School was a five-story building on the Upper West Side. The top four floors jutted out over the ground floor, and immense glass walls were framed by willowy cement panels. Marla's mother had chosen this particular private school for her because a lot of teenagers who had budding and sometimes famous careers went there. It was rarely a problem for a student to arrange to have a week or two off to work on a shoot, act in a movie, or go to a tennis tournament, like Kyla Recki, Marla's best friend.

When Marla stepped from the taxi in front of her school, snowflakes floated in the cold air and gathered in delicate swirls. A winter wind whipped down the street and over the sidewalks, an unwelcome presence that entered the city, hostile to spring. The tulips in the narrow beds in front of the school looked stiff and vulnerable, almost frozen.

Marla's homework was waiting in a message box at the principal's office, a two-inch stack of handouts to be read, and several take-home tests to do. Kyla Recki came in just as Marla was looking through her assignments. Kyla's blue eyes were bright, and a smile beamed from ear to ear.

"See you in two weeks!" she said happily by way of greeting, reaching for a stack of papers in an adjoining box.

"Two weeks?" Marla looked at Kyla, puzzled.

"Sure. Tomorrow I go to Canada for Tom McKenna's tennis clinic. I told you weeks ago I was accepted. He's taking half a dozen of the best players from the Junior Tennis Federation for ten days of tips and training."

Marla bit her lower lip and began stuffing her homework assignments into her nylon knapsack. "I remember now. Tom McKenna is tennis's bad boy."

Kyla brushed her medium-length silky blond hair away from her eyes. "Yeah, the one who curses the referees and throws his tennis racquet at reporters.

But he's the best in the world. As of tomorrow, I'm out of here."

"I hoped we could have a study session this weekend," Marla sighed. She glanced at the homework assignment from her mathematics class before putting it in the knapsack. "I'm lost in trig, Kyla."

Kyla thought a moment. "How about tonight. I have to pack, but—"

Marla's shoulders sagged. "I promised my friend Barbara I'd go out with her on a blind date."

"And you're worried about trigonometry?" Kyla said in a tone that was mildly disapproving.

"It's my chance to meet Cubbie Cube."

"The rap singer?" Kyla rolled her eyes. "Marla, you're turning into a club kid," she teased, referring to the wandering band of New York teenagers and rich kids that seemed to live their entire lives in one nightclub or another. "Or even worse, a groupie like Barbara."

"Hardly," Marla insisted. "And even if it were true, so what? Models are supposed to lead glamorous lives. I mean, everyone thinks I do anyway, so I might as well live up to the image."

Kyla nodded toward the pile of work in Marla's hands. "How're you going to get that done?"

"When I get home tonight," Marla assured her. She would too, if it took her until two o'clock in the morning.

"Ever think about sleeping?"

"Kyla!"

"Okay, okay." Kyla put her arms up, as if to fend off Marla's exasperation. "I promise not to get after you. Look, I'll drop my trig notes off at your place after I finish with them tonight. That way you'll have them while I'm away. I'm sure not going to need them up in Canada."

Marla looked relieved. "Kyla, you're like a rock. I don't know what I'd do without you."

Kyla gave her a hug. "Best friends."

"Forever." Marla smiled, thankful for the quick embrace.

Skipping dinner was not a problem. Marla's mother was drinking a second martini and had already forgotten about eating. Mrs. Drake was an older version of her daughter, petite and dark-haired. As a young woman, she'd had a brief career as an actress. Then she married a busy attorney, had Marla, and devoted herself to her daughter. Marla owed her modeling career to her mother's show business connections.

Marla was little more than three months old when she played a newborn in a baby food commercial. At the age of five her face was famous from coast to coast as the precocious dark-haired little girl who loved a certain brand of pickles. There had been an endless regimen of ballet classes, tap, singing, piano, and drama lessons, and her mother led her around to endless call-ups and auditions in the crazy backstage world of the Broadway theater.

When Marla was eight she landed a major part in a musical. Her mother's ambition had been realized. Unfortunately, reviews were terrible. The show closed two weeks later. Marla would never forget the day it happened. It seemed as if the bottom had fallen out of the world for Mrs. Drake. She started drinking.

After Marla's stage career as a child actress stumbled, modeling work picked up. She went from playing a precocious little girl to a rambunctious adolescent. She rarely bothered with posing for catalogues or book covers, working mainly in television commercials.

And Marla worked. Long days in the studios, then long, late nights doing her schoolwork, and maintaining her grades. While her mother bragged to friends that Marla never even had to study, Marla kept secret all the times she worked quietly in her room into the wee hours of the morning, the sliver of light that escaped beneath the door blocked by a rolled-up towel.

Marla was a perfect student and a perfect daughter. She was determined to make up for what happened when she was eight. Her mother would never be disappointed in her again. And someday, maybe she would even stop drinking.

A year earlier Marla made the cover of *Cheeky* magazine, and last month she'd been shot for the cover of *Vogue*. Her career had picked up momentum and catapulted her to the top. But Mrs. Drake still lost herself in her five o'clock martinis. She stood in the living room doorway, watching Marla hang her coat in the foyer.

"Your father's going to be late from the office again," Mrs. Drake purred between sips of vodka and vermouth. "He has a big case coming up in court."

Marla could never tell if her mother was being sarcastic, ironic, or naive enough to believe that her father was really at the office, working late. Marla had known since she was fifteen that Mr. Drake had affairs with other women. She had always loved to smell his jackets when he hung them in the hall closet. One day she began to notice blond hairs on the fabric. And then, in a pocket once, an airplane ticket in another woman's name. It was something she had never mentioned to either of her parents, or even to Kyla, as if by not saying it out loud, it could not possibly be true.

"I'm going out tonight," Marla announced. "Barbara, one of the girls at Snap! asked me to meet her for dinner."

Mrs. Drake smiled unsteadily, and leaned against the door frame. "Just the two of you?" Her words were a little slurred, loose around the edges. "Or are you meeting some boys? A girl your age should have a boyfriend."

"Mother, you know I'm between boyfriends," Marla said evasively. Boyfriends were a problem for her. It wasn't that she didn't get lots of offers, only that the guys she picked to go out with always seemed to turn out to be jerks. She hoisted the little knapsack filled with her homework assignments and headed down the long hall.

"What about your studies?" Mrs. Drake called out almost automatically.

"Consider them done," Marla said lightly just before she disappeared into her bedroom.

Marla wolfed down another chocolate bar for the energy the sugar in it would give her. She disrobed for the shower, and paused to look at herself in the mirror, smoothing her hands along her skin, pinching and rubbing, alert for the least sign that she might be putting on weight. She thought she detected a little thickening along her thigh. In fact, on second look she was sure. She took the last piece of the chocolate bar, hurled it into the toilet, and flushed.

She decided to wear a slinky black dress with a web of tiny dark metallic beads sewn along one hip. It had cost a fortune, but it was the one major luxury she gave herself last year out of her earnings as a model. Actually, it occurred to her, it was her mother's idea.

I look perfect, she thought, examining herself in the mirror after her makeup was on. Picture perfect. But deep inside her another little voice was screaming, *Just like everyone expects you to be.*

CHAPTER 2

The Universal Grill was mobbed, and even the onset of the unusual spring snowstorm didn't stop people from arriving. Marla entered with Barbara, shaking snow from her long, dark hair, and brushing it off the shoulders of her jacket. The blizzard was in full force outside, with cold, driving winds piling snow into drifts along the streets. Patrons were crammed at little tables, along a banquette that lined a wall, and at the stools at the bar. Even the aisles were full of people waiting, calling out to harried waiters, "Party of ten!"

Marla spotted Cubbie Cube waiting at a big table near the front window, surrounded by an entourage of a dozen people. Barbara's face sank when she saw a table full of club kids. She met Marla's eyes and twisted her face to show her displeasure.

"Hey, there's my date, c'mere, babe!" the Cube shouted when he saw Barbara. Around the restaurant, heads turned to see who was joining the rap star's table. They squeezed in and Cubbie Cube draped his arm around Barbara's shoulders. Marla sat next to a guy named Gerry, who said he was the rap singer's press agent. Wearing a baseball cap pulled on back to front, to Marla he looked more like a skateboarder.

The waiter was tall and thin, and for some reason he wore an enormous turban, which seemed strange since the rest of his outfit consisted of blue jeans and a T-shirt. But, Marla knew, that was the kind of thing that got restaurants like the Universal written up in magazines. The waiter took their orders without writing a thing down, even though everyone at the table seemed to be ordering at the same time. As he took the menu from Marla's hand, he caught her eye and winked. "Fasten your seat belt, it's going to be a rough flight," he said.

For Marla, it didn't get rough until dinner was almost over. She excused herself to go to the rest room. When she came out, she glanced across the restaurant and saw her father at a table on the other side. He was having dinner with a young, attractive blond woman.

An accidental witness, Marla froze. The blood drained from her face, leaving her faintly dizzy, and a thud hit her stomach like a fist. She watched her father lean across the table to take the woman's hand in his.

Suddenly, it seemed like everything was coming at Marla at once. The lights in the restaurant grew golden auras. The waiters' clatter and diners' chatter merged into an indistinguishable babble. Marla's eyes filled with tears. Then Cubbie Cube stood in front of her, blocking her view. The rap singer was tall, and muscled from pumping iron, but his brush-cut hair and a leering grin gave him a sinister look.

"Hey, babe." The Cube looked at her as if he expected a kiss.

Without replying, Marla tried to move past him, but he stepped sideways and stopped her.

"It's you I like, babe." His hand fell heavily on her hip, his fingers pressing into her skin.

"Stop it," she protested.

His hand gripped her tighter, and he pulled her toward him. "Why don't we split—"

"Please!" Marla cried, pushing his hand aside and backing away. She felt tears sting her eyes, and knew if she didn't get out of there, she would break down and cry.

"Whatsamatter, babe?" the rap singer persisted, still smiling as if it were all a joke. He reached for her again.

This time Marla planted her hands firmly on his massive chest and tried to shove him away. Cubbie Cube's cool suddenly evaporated, and his eyes darkened with anger.

"Hey!" he growled. "You think you're some hot model, well, babes don't treat me—"

Marla ignored him and slid past. All she focused on was the front door of the restaurant, and the milling crowd she had to pass through to get there.

The rap singer shouted after her. "You're just a stuck-up, anorexic—"

The rest of his taunt was drowned out by the hubbub as Marla fled across the restaurant. She grabbed her coat from her chair as she passed the table crowded with club kids.

"What's up?" Barbara asked, wide-eyed and innocent. "Where's Cubbie?"

Marla didn't stop to answer. She rushed from the restaurant into the cold, driving blizzard outside.

* * *

In the sudden quiet after the noisy restaurant, Marla realized her ears were ringing. The street was white with snow, and icy winds plucked at her collar and wrists. Few cars had ventured out, and no taxis were in sight. The wind howled and rattled against the iron fire escapes that lined the façades of the old brick buildings. No one came outside after her. Marla shivered, pulled her coat closer, and strode toward Seventh Avenue.

Lights glowed from a delicatessen on the corner. Despite having just had dinner, Marla felt hungry, ravenously so, as if she had not eaten in weeks. She knew what was coming, an enormous emptiness inside that would be filled, somehow, only if she binged on sweet things. She wiped tears from the corners of her eyes and went inside. She grabbed two chocolate brownies from a display rack, threw three dollars on the counter, and rushed back outside without waiting for change.

Almost instantly she knew she was being watched again. It was a weird feeling, a kind of ripple up her spine, and a shiver in the back of her neck, the certainty that a pair of eyes gazed at her. Suddenly, floating on an icy breeze, she caught a strange smell, the rank odor of decay, like the stench of sewer gas but somehow different. It held the scent of rotting greenery, which seemed odd in the cold, lifeless air.

She stopped, frozen in her tracks, and felt raw terror sweep over her. She struggled against it and forced herself to turn around. A long, bulky shadow fell across the snow at the corner of the deli, just as it had earlier that day when she left Jean-Michel's studio. Then it vanished. Someone had just moved out of the glow of the streetlight.

Marla's terror was replaced by anger. If someone were following her, some fan who had seen her face on the cover of a magazine, she was going to confront him and put a stop to it once and for all. She strode to the corner and boldly turned it, prepared to face whoever was there.

The street was deserted. She glanced down and saw a footprint in the snow. It was very odd, a large oval shape with a smaller oval like a giant toe. Like orthopedic shoes, she thought. There was more than one. They grew farther and farther apart, as if someone had begun to run up the street.

Then they vanished altogether.

Marla shuddered. She strode back to Seventh Avenue, searching frantically for a taxi. By the time she hailed one, her feet were wet and numb with cold. The backseat of the cab seemed snug and warm, secure against the storm outside. The car sailed uptown through the driving snow and empty Manhattan streets to the apartment building on the Upper West Side where she lived. On the way she devoured one of the brownies, wolfing it down without even tasting it. The taxi driver took a wrong turn on a one-way street, a block from her building.

"Just stop here," Marla said with frustration, dropping the fare into the front seat. She hitched up her skirt and stepped outside, her shoes sinking into several inches of cold, wet snow. The blizzard had abated, but snowflakes still danced and floated in the cold night air. Streetlights glowed overhead, illuminating stretches of snow and patches of black sidewalk where it had already melted. Still, the night seemed darker than usual.

The taxi departed and almost instantly Marla was seized again by the certainty that she was being watched. This time it was stronger than ever. Once again the odd smell of sewer gas strayed past her nostrils, acrid and dark. The street was empty, save for the roiling wind.

The apartment building where she lived was visible at the end of the street. Marla started toward it, glancing back over her shoulder again and again, seeing only the trail made by the delicate imprints of her high-heeled shoes in the damp white snow. She walked faster. Shivers crept up her spine and settled at the back of her neck, a coldness that came from fear, not from the weather. Her heart pounded in her chest. She started to run blindly, the cold air biting at her lungs.

When she turned the corner, she saw the doorman sitting alone in the lobby. She passed him with scarcely a nod. A short elevator ride later she fumbled with her key and pushed inside.

The apartment was dark except for a light from a single lamp in the living room. Marla's mother sat in a wing chair, staring off into space with a strange expression on her face. She wore a flowered dress with too much jewelry, and her lipstick was smudged. An empty cocktail glass sat on the table beside her. String music by Mantovani was playing mindlessly on the stereo. Marla mumbled a quick hello, which her mother barely acknowledged.

She rushed to her room and wolfed down the second brownie while stripping off the black silk dress. Her chest heaved as she tried to control her tears. She couldn't let herself feel anything—it was far too painful. Better to be empty inside, she thought. Better to be a cardboard doll, observing all the rituals with smiles and nods, and a few cool words. Perfect model, perfect student, perfect daughter. Everyone admired Marla Drake and wanted to be just like her.

But it wasn't the truth. The truth was Cubbie Cube's taunt, and the way the rap singer had said it, his voice dripping with contempt for Marla's terrible secret. She really was anorexic, and bulimic too. She spent days eating almost nothing, and then binged, stuffing herself with sugar and sweets. Then she threw it all up, and felt even less real inside. To everyone she was a walking, talking, picture-perfect teenage glamour model, but Marla Drake felt hollow.

She went into her bathroom and turned on the faucet. Cold water gushed into the sink. Quickly, Marla filled a tall glass and gulped it down. She drank two more, set the glass on the counter, and knelt before the toilet in a posture almost of prayer. She knew exactly where to press her finger on the back of her tongue. She'd been doing it almost two years. Her stomach heaved. Somewhere far away, so distant it seemed to come from another planet, she heard a doorbell ring.

Kyla Recki arrived at Marla's apartment building only a few minutes after Marla had, her trigonometry notes in a canvas bag under her arm. The doorman recognized her, and told her that Marla had come in only a few minutes before.

Kyla was surprised. It was early for her friend to be back. Mrs. Drake opened the door. She smelled of vodka, even though vodka was not supposed to have a smell. To Kyla it was unmistakable—icy. Like the chill beneath the wind outside. Besides, an empty cocktail glass rested on a polished wood side table.

"My daughter's in her room," Mrs. Drake said sullenly, waving her toward Marla's bedroom. Without another word she walked back to the living room, staggering slightly on her heels.

Kyla knocked lightly on the wooden door, waited a moment without an answer, then tried the handle. It was unlocked. She opened it and walked in. A column of light glowed from the partly open door to Marla's bathroom.

Kyla hesitated and called out. She threw her canvas bag onto the bed and slipped into the bathroom. Marla was crumpled on the floor, her head resting on the toilet seat, weeping relentlessly. A stream of cold water gushed into the sink from the open faucet.

"Marla!" Kyla knelt beside her friend as Marla looked up, her face swollen, her eyes red, the tracks of her tears etched down her cheeks.

"I was followed," Marla sobbed. "Someone followed me home. They were following me before today too."

"Oh, Marla" was all Kyla could say, hugging her friend tightly. She got up, turned off the faucet, and opened the window to air out the small bathroom. She helped Marla into the bedroom, then went back and flushed the toilet.

"Should I call the police?" Kyla asked.

Marla sat on her bed, a small, crumpled figure, shivering in her housecoat. She shrugged. "I never saw anyone really. I just . . . I know someone was watching me. And following. But I never saw anyone."

Kyla sat down on the bed beside Marla, slipped her arm around her shoulders, and pulled her close. Marla spilled out the story of her evening. When she was finished she looked at Kyla.

"Seeing my father with his girlfriend," Marla sniffed, and gave a small, weary laugh. "Well, it's not as if I hadn't expected it." She sighed unhappily. "It's different when something you know about is suddenly right there in the flesh though."

"And Cubbie Cube's boorishness just made matters worse," said Kyla. "I don't blame you for being upset."

"So now you know," Marla said. She nodded her head toward the open bathroom door.

"I knew," Kyla answered simply. "At least, I kind of thought, sometimes, that you—"

"Sometimes I don't know who I am anymore, Kyla," Marla interrupted. "I mean, everyone thinks I have it all, and I guess I do, but I feel totally empty inside, like everything I do is just to please people. And so I go crazy and stuff myself full of junk food and chocolate bars. Like if I eat, I can fill myself up. But afterward I can't stand having all that junk inside, so I want to be empty again."

Kyla was silent for a moment, and then she said, "Marla? Why don't you come away with me?"

Marla looked curiously at her best friend. "I thought you were going to Canada tomorrow for a tennis clinic."

Kyla nodded. "To a big resort hotel on a lake, where there's nothing to do except swim and play tennis. Come with me," she urged. "You're totally stressed out to the point where you're getting paranoid. You can get the time off school easily enough if you tell them you're doing a photo shoot somewhere. It's only for ten days."

Marla was silent. She slouched against Kyla, wondering if it was a good idea or not.

Without saying another word Kyla reached for the telephone on the bedside table. She pressed in a number. Marla looked up at her with a questioning look on her face.

"It's the airline company," Kyla explained. "Let's see if we can get you a ticket."

CHAPTER 3

Winter, Part II, as the tabloids dubbed it, vanished as quickly as it had arrived. By Wednesday morning the driving blizzard gave way to blue skies, a warm yellow sun, and mounds of snow steadily melting into the gutters. The storm sewers were clogged with slush, and black, oily pools of water spread into the intersections, adding to New York City's general confusion.

When the airport car pulled up in front of Marla's building at nine-thirty, Kyla saw her waiting under the awning that stretched from the doors to the curb. The sidewalk in front of her building had been cleaned of snow and generously salted.

Kyla leaned over in the backseat, pulled up the handle, and pushed the door open, while Marla skipped across a runnel of water and climbed inside. She had bags under her eyes from a restless night. Her sleep had been filled with strange, turbulent dreams. One she remembered.

She had been standing in a room in a tower made of logs. There were windows on every side and brilliant blue sky beyond, but there was no door into the room, and the air was cold as ice. A man stood before her, stoop-shouldered with a small round head that bobbed strangely on his massive shoulders. He stretched his arms out and opened his hands. Diamonds and sapphires, topazes and emeralds cascaded between his open fingers onto the floor, glinting like chunks of colored ice. She remembered feeling terrified but also wanting those jewels more than anything else in her life. She couldn't remember anything else from the dream.

"I can't believe I'm doing this," Marla told Kyla, pulling her enormous handbag into the car after her. Outside, the driver opened the trunk and placed her suitcase inside.

"What did your mother say?" Kyla asked.

"I left a note," Marla gulped guiltily. "Well, she was still asleep," she added, her voice rising slightly as if in protest.

Kyla smiled with mock sweetness. "Did I say anything?"

"I'll call her from the airport," Marla decided. "It's not as if she cares."

"Whatever," Kyla said vaguely.

Marla sank back into her seat, pulling her coat around her tightly, and stared out the window as the car pulled into traffic. Their flight to Minneapolis left at eleven o'clock, and they made it to the airplane with little time to spare. Five hours later—minus two when they crossed time zones—they flew from Minneapolis to Winnipeg, Manitoba.

Marla plucked the flight magazine from the pouch in

front of her seat and opened it to a map of the continent. She stared at the route they were on with distaste. Winnipeg was a two-hour flight across the Canadian border almost due north of Minneapolis, and a few hundred miles west of Lake Superior, the westernmost of the Great Lakes.

"I've been to some out-of-the-way places for modeling," Marla muttered. "But if we go any farther we're falling off the edge of the earth."

"Yeah, out-of-the-way places," Kyla said sarcastically. "In the Caribbean. In Europe."

"Is this Lake of the Woods?" Marla pointed to a large, long lake sprawling up the center of the Canadian province of Manitoba.

Kyla shook her head. "Lake Winnipeg," she corrected. She leaned over the map and pointed to Lake Winnipeg and Lake Superior, both of which were the size of inland seas. Between the two great bodies of water and connected by rivers was a smaller lake.

"That's Lake of the Woods. Kenora, the town we're going to, is on the lake, just across the border of Manitoba in the province of Ontario."

"And now they do tennis clinics in—what's this place called, here?"

"Kenora," Kyla laughed, reaching under her seat for her bag.

"Kenowhere, as far as I'm concerned." Marla sighed.

"Tom McKenna is one of the sexiest, richest tennis stars in the world. Everywhere he goes there are about a zillion groupies traipsing after him. So he chose this place because it's totally lost." Kyla dug a brochure out of her purse and handed it to Marla. "The Keewatin Lodge," she announced.

On the cover of the glossy pamphlet was an enormous fortresslike building constructed entirely of logs. A vast central tower was flanked by numerous wings, each five stories high. The logs, skinned of their bark and varnished, had been laid in different criss-crossing patterns. It was set amid rolling green lawns, with a thick pine forest on one side, and a deep blue lake beyond.

Marla felt a strange chill fluttering at the back of her neck. She knew the place. It was definitely familiar. At the same time, she knew she had never seen it before.

"Keewatin is the name of the Indian spirit of the north wind," Kyla explained. "It's a luxury hotel, built about eighty years ago."

"How do you know all this," Marla asked, flipping the leaflet open.

"Extra sensory perception," Kyla said with light sarcasm. "And reading the brochure helped too."

By the time the airplane arrived over Winnipeg, the sun was a great red orb descending rapidly toward the western horizon. Below, a checkerboard of wheat fields sprawled in the gathering purple dusk. The city's lights glimmered in the twilight, pinned like a diamond brooch upon the dark, flat surface of the prairie.

Marla and Kyla spent the night at a hotel near the airport on the northern edge of the city. The next morning, a DC-9 waited on the runway. They gathered briefly in the terminal lounge with a dozen other passengers—a man in a business suit, a native family with two quiet young children, two bearded Hutterite men in old-fashioned black suits, two loud-talking Texas ranchers who owned a fishing camp and—

"One hunky guy," Marla stated succinctly, murmuring into Kyla's ear. She was glancing across the sterile waiting room at a tall, handsome teenager. He was blond, and heavily tanned despite the early spring season. His suitcase rested on the floor beside him, but he gripped an expensive leather racquet case in his hand. Crossed tennis racquets were embroidered over the breast pocket of his blue nylon jacket. "Is he a part of the tennis clinic?"

"I've never seen him," Kyla said, scrutinizing the tall, slender teenager. She was curious and mildly surprised. McKenna's tennis clinic was limited to six amateurs who were on the verge of going pro. Kyla had already played with or against every one of them at one tournament or another. Except for this guy.

An airline employee opened the doors leading to the runway and announced they were ready to board. Passengers flowed onto the open tarmac, walking the fifty-foot stretch to the airplane.

Marla and Kyla found their seats in the middle. The handsome blond boarded and caught Marla's eye. He came down the aisle, beaming at them, and gestured toward Kyla's racquet case.

"Are we going to the same place?" he asked, checking his boarding pass and slipping into the seat in front of them.

"The Keewatin," Marla said before Kyla could answer. "Tom McKenna's clinic." She paused. "Well, Kyla is. I'm Marla Drake."

"Kyla Recki," Kyla offered.

"Mark Lorrington. I'm in McKenna's clinic too."

The three teenagers shook hands all around. Marla found Mark's looks quite dazzling. He had chiseled features and a dimpled chin, short blond hair, and strong arms. He wore chinos and a light green shirt.

"We're from New York," Marla said. "You?"

"Santa Monica, California," Mark replied.

"I thought I knew all the other kids in the clinic," Kyla began tentatively.

"So what am I doing here, right?" Mark Lorrington answered quickly. "My dad's one of the owners of the Keewatin, so he pulled a few strings."

"Lucky you," Marla commented, glancing at Kyla.

"I'm a pretty awesome tennis player anyway. I'm going pro next year. Two years from now I'll rule the courts."

"You're pretty sure of that," Kyla commented.

Mark smiled boldly and nodded. "Yup. Because I'm used to getting what I want." His smile deepened and he looked at Marla. "And you? Tennis too?"

Marla shook her head. "I just came along for the ride." She looked at Kyla. "Just for the ride."

The DC-9 began to taxi down the runway. Moments later it ascended into the vast dome of blue sky. In the bright sunlight the geometric patterns of wheat fields, brown and yellow in the early spring before the planting, sprawled to the horizon like a great quilt, outlined by roads and highways that ran straight as arrows to the edge of the earth. Sprinkled here and there across the landscape were tiny buildings—barns and farmhouses. The DC-9 headed east-northeast.

"You guys ever been this far north before?" Mark asked, turning in his seat to speak to Marla and Kyla.

Marla shook her head. "Are you kidding? This is interplanetary travel to me."

Mark laughed. "Yeah, it's pretty out of the way. I've been coming up here since I was a kid. It's fun in the summer when the Keewatin's full of people from Europe and all over the States." He pointed out the DC-9's window. "Look, you can see where the prairie turns into the Canadian Shield."

At the edge of the earth the wheat fields ended abruptly and a forest began, a great swath of evergreens, fields of bare gray rock, splotches of white and brown where the leaves had not yet come out on aspens and birches. As the airplane flew on, Marla began to see lakes, hundreds of them, dotting the wilderness landscape as far as her eye could see. The Canadian north looked to be more water than earth.

Half an hour later the primeval forest spread around the shores of an enormous blue lake. Dozens of islands dotted its surface, and a large town of low-rise buildings congregated on the far shore. The DC-9 descended, skimming over the roofs of cottages and camps built along the lake. Several modern high-rises stood in a row by the water's edge, where long wooden piers jutted into the water. Airplanes on pontoons bobbed on the surface of the lake.

"Biggest town in two hundred miles in either direction," Mark announced matter-of-factly.

"Kenowhere," Marla said, her heart sinking at the first sight of the lonely outpost. She turned to Kyla. "Well, you promised me a week of nothing to do."

The DC-9 landed at a small airport on the outskirts of Kenora, and the passengers disembarked, walking across the tarmac to the terminal.

Marla stepped from the plane, negotiated the short steps, and planted her feet firmly on the ground. The terminal was a small one-story affair with a single glass tower. Beyond it and the runway stretched an unbroken wall of wild green spruce trees, trunks askew and branches tangled.

"Tyrone!" Mark yelled.

Marla looked in the direction Mark was waving. A tall, handsome teenager with chestnut hair stood outside the sliding glass doors, a bright smile beaming across his olive face.

"My friend Tyrone," Mark called back to Marla and Kyla. "He's our ride to the Keewatin!"

CHAPTER

At the terminal building the dark-haired teenager strode forward and greeted Mark with the warm embrace of an old friend.

Mark introduced him to Marla and Kyla. "Tyrone Wiloski. His mom owns the gift shop at the Keewatin."

"And I run the airport shuttle when no one else is around," Tyrone added, flashing a warm smile at the girls.

Tyrone was taller than Mark, and lanky where Mark was muscled and stocky. And his skin was olive, as dark as Mark's suntan, but naturally so. His eyebrows almost met in the middle, framing eyes that were deep gray, the color of charcoal.

"You must be here for McKenna's tennis clinic," Tyrone motioned toward Kyla's racket case.

Kyla nodded. "I'm Kyla Recki. And this is Marla Drake. We phoned yesterday about—"

"An extra room at the inn." Tyrone smiled. "I was

working behind the desk when you called. Considering the Keewatin has about a ninety percent vacancy rate in the off season, they managed to squeeze you in. So welcome to the great northern forest. You guys are the first to arrive. McKenna and the other kids are all flying in tomorrow."

Tyrone led them through the small airport terminal, where they waited for their baggage.

"Do you work full-time at the hotel?" Marla asked.

"Until I go to university in the fall," Tyrone told her. "I picked up some summer courses last year and finished all my high school credits at Christmas. What about you?"

"The school I go to is flexible," Marla answered vaguely.

When their bags came, Tyrone picked up the two heaviest ones and led the group to a station wagon parked at the curb out front. The name of the Keewatin was painted on the door panels. Overhead, the sky was deep blue, dotted by popcorn clouds, warmed by the yellow sun. Still, there was an odd chill to the breeze that blew from the spruce forest growing along the edge of the road. Marla took a deep breath.

"The air's so fresh here," she commented. And it was, cool and pure, leavened by the resinous scent of evergreens.

"Not like New York, eh?" Tyrone cracked, placing the suitcases in the back of the station wagon.

"Eh?" Mark teased, slugging Tyrone on the shoulder. He looked at Marla and Kyla and winked. "Tyrone's Canadian, eh? We've known each other since we were little kids, eh, and I used to come up here in the summer." Mark paused. "Eh?" he added again in an exaggerated voice.

Tyrone blushed slightly beneath his dark complexion. "Don't start," he pleaded. Looking at the two girls, he smiled shyly. "His studliness gets carried away by my hokey Canadian accent."

Mark smirked. "That's right, eh, dude."

Tyrone explained that it was a twenty-minute drive from the airport to the hotel. He drove along a road that ran straight through the forest. Spruce trees grew thickly together, like an impenetrable fence of tangled green. The occasional stretch of white-barked birches had bare branches covered with tiny buds.

"I hear you had a bit of winter down in New York City," Tyrone said, turning to glance at Kyla and Marla, who rode in the backseat.

"Almost eight inches of snow," Marla confirmed. "And it froze too, just when all the flowers were about to bud. It never happens at this time of year."

"Well, I hope you didn't bring Old Man Winter back up here with you. We've just been through the longest, coldest winter on record. It was epic."

The car turned along a curve in the road, and Lake of the Woods came into view, its sapphire surface dotted with dozens of small tree-covered islands. Across the lake, the town of Kenora squatted on the shore, a collection of old redbrick and ugly modern buildings climbing the gentle slope away from the water. Beyond, the spruce forest pressed in relentlessly. There was something inexpressively wild and remote about the landscape. It was unlike anything Marla had ever seen.

"I've never been so far north," she said. "What do people do around here?"

"Fish, trap animals for furs, mine, shop," said Tyrone.

"And a lot of rich Texans have fishing camps up in the boonies," Mark piped up. He pointed toward the lake, where a small armada of pontoon planes bobbed on the surface of the placid water. "They go in and out on those planes because there're no roads."

"And the whole area is dotted with reservations," Tyrone added. "Ojibway, mostly."

"Drunk, mostly," Mark snickered derisively. "The Indians all go to Kenora, where they reel in doorways and stagger up and down the streets."

"And freeze to death in winter," Tyrone added quickly to change Mark's drift. "By the way, in Canada we call them native people, not Indians."

"I think it's terrible the way Indians, I mean native people, are treated," Kyla said, folding her arms across her chest.

Tyrone glanced back at her and Marla. "Me too. Three hundred years ago European culture hits Stone Age North America like a collision between a tank and a bicycle. The worst end up on skid row. But on the reservations a lot of native people are trying to preserve their culture."

"What culture?" Mark sneered. "It's just a bunch of superstition. Like the curse of the Keewatin. It's primitive."

"A curse?" Kyla exclaimed, suddenly intrigued.

"That's one thing Mark's father doesn't let them put in the Keewatin's brochures," Tyrone commented.

Marla laughed. "Like there's never a thirteenth floor in a New York apartment building."

"Or anywhere," Tyrone added.

"Tell us about this curse," Kyla demanded. "Is there a ghost or something?"

"Not really," Tyrone said slowly.

"There's a wendigo!" Mark piped up.

Tyrone gave an exasperated sigh. He glanced back at Marla and Kyla. "You should never say that word out loud."

"What word?" Marla asked, puzzled.

"Wendigo." Mark laughed, casting Tyrone a defiant look. A thin smile spread across his face. "It's a cannibal monster that the Indians believe in."

"Native people," Kyla quietly corrected him.

Mark ignored her. "It lives in the forest, and has enormous feet, each with only a single toe. And it runs so fast that it leaves the ground and flies."

"It's fourteen feet high and covered with hair," Tyrone interjected. "And the hair is matted with moss and dead swamp vegetation. It has eyes that roll in blood, razor-sharp antlers sprouting from its forehead, teeth like steak knives, and lips that have been eaten away by parasites. It stinks of swamps and rotting vegetation and dead things. And its heart and skeleton are made of ice."

"A cannibal too," said Marla with sarcasm. "How charming."

"Whenever it can get human flesh," Mark added flatly. "It swoops down from the sky, grabs you, and leaps back up again. It flies so high and so fast that your feet and hands freeze and your eyes get bloodshot. If it doesn't eat you, it freezes your heart and turns you into a wendigo. Then you take on the wendigo's powers and start eating people too."

"So what's all this got to do with the Keewatin?" Marla demanded.

"According to local legend, the mother of all wendigos haunts the land the Keewatin Lodge is built on," Mark explained.

"There was a village there once," Tyrone added. "But for some reason the native people abandoned the site. Even when the *couriers de bois* arrived a hundred years ago, the natives wouldn't go near the place. They claimed a wendigo lived there."

"*Couriers de* what?" Marla asked.

"*Couriers de bois*," Kyla said. "It's French for runners-of-the-wood. It means fur traders and explorers. We learned about them in fifth grade."

"And you remembered?" Marla said, glancing at Kyla incredulously.

"Fur traders used to travel by canoe from Montreal to Hudson Bay. And Lake of the Woods is on the route," Tyrone explained. "They built a trading post where the native village had been. But there are stories of a strange illness, maybe typhoid or cholera or something, that decimated the traders and settlers. Of course, the native people blamed it on the wendigo. So the site was abandoned and Kenora was built farther up the lake."

"The land sat empty until 1910," said Mark. "Then my grandfather bought it and decided to build the Keewatin. He couldn't get any Indians to work there because they claimed the site is still cursed."

"It's still impossible to get native people to work at the Keewatin," Tyrone added.

" 'Cept for Weird Sylvain." Mark laughed. He turned around to face Marla and Kyla. "Sylvain's *métis*—half Indian, half white. He does odd jobs around the Keewatin. We started calling him Weird Sylvain when we were kids. The Indians around here say he saw the wendigo once. And that he's possessed."

"Like in *The Exorcist?*" Marla wondered.

Mark shrugged. "Mind control?" he suggested. "Hypnotism?" He'd never really thought about the mechanics of it.

"Sylvain was a trapper years ago before he started working at the hotel," Tyrone told them. "So I think he went a little crazy on his long winter trips."

"Yeah, but his fingers and ears and the tip of his nose are all shriveled. And his feet are so deformed, he always wears big, strange shoes."

"From frostbite," Tyrone pointed out, "which is pretty normal in the forest in weather that's forty degrees below zero every day." He glanced back at Marla and Kyla. "It's called bush fever up here. Trappers are in the forest for months at a time without seeing any people. After a while they start to hallucinate. Nowadays psychologists say it's because of sensory deprivation. The traditional native explanation is that a person has seen a wendigo. Sometimes when they return to civilization they suffer from bad frostbite and terrible hunger, too, if there's been nothing to eat. According to the legend, though, the frostbite happens because that person has been flying with the wendigo high in the sky."

"Yeah, but they're so hungry they start eating other people in their villages," Mark added.

"That's only in the most extreme cases," Tyrone said. "Even the native people consider it a kind of madness when someone gets to that stage. And Sylvain never ate anyone."

"As far as we know," Mark said. He started doing an imitation of Sylvain, thrusting his shoulders up around his ears, pursing his lips, bugging out his eyes, and shifting crazily.

"Oh, great," said Marla, turning to Kyla. "We're on our way to a haunted Indian hunting ground with a curse on it, a hunchback named Weird Sylvain works there, and this is supposed to be an escape from New York."

"Hey, it's not a grade B film. No one's really ever seen a wendigo. And Sylvain is just weird, right, Tyrone?"

Tyrone had become quite silent.

"Right?" Mark persisted.

"Right," Tyrone said limply. He started to say something, then hesitated. Finally, after a moment, he spoke. "I was going to wait till later to tell you, Mark, but Sylvain disappeared a week ago and the Mounties are looking for him."

"Sylvain?" Mark seemed surprised. "He probably just wandered into the woods for a while."

Tyrone nodded. "Well, he was acting weirder and weirder all winter, and he started looking like hell."

"Worse than usual?"

Tyrone nodded.

"Maybe he saw the wendigo again," Mark suggested lightly.

"I thought you aren't supposed to say that name out loud?" Marla said.

Mark nodded. "Because if the wendigo hears its name out loud—" He made his voice sound eerie. "It comes for you!"

There was a moment of uncomfortable silence. "Here we are!" Tyrone announced. "On the left."

Behind a thick forest of tall spruce trees rose the log towers of the great hotel. The station wagon drove through a stone gate. A row of pine trees pressed against the drive on either side. Half a mile later the forest opened up to a grand view of Lake of the Woods, and the Keewatin Lodge in the foreground.

It was set in the middle of a vast green lawn, with copses of white-barked birch trees and tall, old pines growing along the lakeshore. Tyrone pulled up a circular drive to the great front doors and came to a stop.

Marla stepped from the car into warm sunlight, stretching, her eyes drawn upward to the roof of the immense hotel. Rows of tiny windows were set in overhanging shingled gables. Below, log walls rose four stories, with rows of green-shuttered windows. Once again the strange sense of déjà vu that she felt on the airplane when she looked at the brochure struck her. She was certain that she had seen this building once before.

What Marla noticed most intensely, though, was the silence. Beyond the sounds of slamming car doors, chatter, the breezes zithering through the needled boughs of nearby pines, the distant murmur of waves lapping at the shore, her heels scraping on the asphalt drive, there was a stillness that was almost unnerving.

She turned and saw a police car parked outside a small log building across the driveway from the hotel. A sign read EMPLOYEES ONLY.

"RCMP," Tyrone said, getting out of the driver's seat and following her glance. "That's the office. They must be seeing Mr. Purcell, the manager. Maybe they found Sylvain."

"Remember, the Mounties always get their man," Mark said, walking around the front of the car.

"You mean the Royal Canadian Mounted Police?" Kyla asked.

"Yup," said Mark. "The one and only."

Tyrone started around to the back of the car for the luggage just as two policemen in khaki green uniforms and nylon duffel coats left the log building and walked toward their car.

"I thought they wore red uniforms and Smokey the Bear hats," Marla said, gazing after them with evident disappointment.

A pale, thin man in a doorman's uniform appeared at the top of the steps and hurried down to the car.

"Hey, René. What's up?" Tyrone greeted the man. He gestured with his head and lugged Marla's big suitcase out of the rear of the station wagon.

"They're here about Sylvain," the doorman replied, keeping his voice low. He took a suitcase from Tyrone and his eyes glinted conspiratorially. "Mounties went up to his cabin at Four Mile Point."

Marla heard them speaking, but the words drifted in the background.

"They found a body there, and it wasn't Sylvain's," the man named René continued. "What was left of it anyway. Now they want him for murder."

"Sounds like Sylvain saw the wendigo after all," Mark said.

Barely listening, Marla walked slowly toward the Keewatin, her gaze drawn upward to the high log walls and the shuttered windows. She realized suddenly why it seemed familiar. It was the dream she'd had the restless night before she left New York. She remembered the high, windswept tower of logs surrounded by blue sky, the strange little man, jewels pouring through his hands like colored ice. This is where the dream took place! Somehow, she was certain. She heard the doorman finish his tale with apparent relish.

"Guess he did see the wendigo. Them human bones they found were gnawed on, eh. Looks like old Sylvain got mighty hungry."

CHAPTER 5

Marla stood in the lobby of the Keewatin Lodge, gazing up at a cathedral of logs that soared three stories to a beamed ceiling. The sides were lined with timber balconies, and hung with pennants and flags. Rows of plush, overstuffed sofas and chairs were dwarfed by the height of the room. The plank floors had been polished to a sheen and covered with long Persian rugs, worn and slightly faded by the traffic of feet over many years.

On one side stood a great rock fireplace with a hearth taller than she was. Opposite, and tucked under the low ceiling of one of the wings, was a huge oak desk. Kyla went to register for both of them while Marla wandered across the lobby. She saw a gift shop with two large display windows tucked under some log posts. The name of the shop, the Gracious Loon, was painted over a scene of pine trees and a beautiful blue lake. On one side several black and white checkered water birds floated on the lake. In the upper left-hand corner a strange Indian being, his figure blurred, swept over the tops of the trees like the wind.

"Are you one of those kids here for McKenna's tennis clinic?" a woman's voice called out. Marla turned and saw an attractive woman watching her from behind a cash register just inside the Gracious Loon's open door. She had long dark-brown hair, which she tied back with a paisley scarf, and wore a loose-fitting blouse over a peasant skirt. Heavy copper bracelets jangled at her wrists. A zodiac sign, Aquarius, hung from a chain at her neck. The woman smiled.

"Off season we don't have many guests," she said to explain her question. "Especially young people. So I figured . . ."

"My friend is," Marla said, waving vaguely in the direction Kyla had gone. "We're from New York. I just came for . . ." Marla stumbled. She still wasn't sure what she was doing in Kenora, Ontario. "For a vacation. I'm Marla Drake."

"Vivian." She gestured at the shop. "Proud owner."

The Gracious Loon was crammed with souvenirs and memorabilia of the north: Indian dolls in suede dresses, great diodes of amethysts, felt pennants and T-shirts, rainbow stickers, translucent plastic butterflies, and ashtrays hand-painted with scenes of mountain lakes, teaspoons with tiny imprints of the Keewatin Lodge, mottled green pottery in grotesque shapes, bags of scented leaves, and a rack of snow globes.

Marla took it all in with one sweeping glance and suppressed a sigh. Shopping was not going to be easy in Kenora. She pointed at the Gracious Loon sign and the strange figure whose legs dissolved in a blur of speed. "Who is that supposed to be?"

"That's Keewatin, the spirit of the north wind." Cryptically, Vivian added in a low voice, "And between poor old Sylvain and that Willie Beaver case last year, Keewatin's been blowing hard in these parts."

"You want to scare her back to New York on her first day?" Tyrone stood in the doorway of the Gracious Loon, glaring at Vivian. "She just got here."

Marla saw the resemblance immediately. "You're brother and sister!"

Tyrone scowled and began to blush. He sauntered slowly into the shop. "My mother, actually."

Vivian was unperturbed. She smiled at Marla. "It's true. I spawned this creature seventeen and a half years ago."

Marla looked at Tyrone, who was scowling. His eyes seemed even darker, like stormclouds crossing a sun, she thought. She hated to admit it, but she found his discomfort with his mother funny, and she couldn't help smiling.

"I doubt you need to hear any more bizarre tales of the north," Tyrone told Marla.

"I was just referring to an old native legend," Vivian said casually. "What with this news about Sylvain, it's made us all jumpy."

"About this monster called the wendigo?" Marla ventured.

Vivian nodded. "The native legend is that once a great sorcerer cut open his veins. Keewatin, the cold north wind, blew into his blood and froze his heart. And the sorcerer became the first wendigo."

Her hand moved to the zodiac sign around her neck, and she rubbed it absentmindedly with a nervous laugh. "Well, the natives around here have been avoiding Sylvain for years because they say he's seen the wendigo. And as I was saying, there's that native trapper named Willie Beaver who ate his wife and children, and ran off into the wilderness. He's another one they say saw the wendigo, and he worked here for a season before he ran off."

Tyrone's eyes grew dark, the light draining from them.

"I thought you weren't supposed to say its name out loud," Marla pointed out.

He shrugged with studied carelessness. "Well, talking about it's one thing," he muttered darkly. "But I wouldn't go shouting it from the treetops either."

Marla and Kyla had adjoining rooms on the third floor with views overlooking the terrace restaurant, which was dotted with table umbrellas like a field of colored mushrooms. The lake, at the edge of the green lawns, looked cold and blue, its rippling waves glinting in late afternoon sunlight.

In Marla's room there was an enormous bed, like something from "Goldilocks and the Three Bears," a humongous contraption of maple posts and a high wooden headboard. Like everything else at the Keewatin, the walls were made of logs. The chairs were upholstered in English chintz. Rich burgundy drapes hung at the windows, their elegance contrasting with rusticity.

What really surprised Marla was the old-fashioned bathroom with its enormous porcelain fixtures, a pedestal sink, and a grand old tub. A shower stall had been added beside the toilet. The taps were burnished with age, and the towel racks were porcelain. The walls shone with white tile, and there were two art deco wall sconces on either side of the enormous mirror.

She stopped there, stepped back, and examined her

reflection, testing her hips, her breasts, her rear. She thought she looked a little heavy, and vowed to diet for the next few days. To Marla, dieting meant not eating.

So now you're here, she thought. What next? Well, there was always Mark Lorrington, the little voice in the back of her mind whispered deliciously amid the sound of mental alarm bells that she wanted to ignore. Mark was a bit full of himself, but he was cute too. Her feelings excited her and frightened her at the same time. As always when anxiety struck, she felt hungry.

Marla threw her suitcase open on the bed and rummaged in the liner for a box of cookies she had packed. She was just about to give in to temptation when there was a tap at the door. She jammed the box in a dresser drawer and went to the door.

Kyla slipped into the room. Disappointment was written across her face like a billboard. "Guess what I just found out! McKenna dislocated his shoulder at a tournament in Florida today. He's canceling the entire weekend, and starting the clinic on Monday instead."

Marla looked at her blankly. "When did that happen?"

"I just got a call from the hotel manager."

Marla shrugged indifferently. "Do you get a refund?"

"That's not the point. We're stuck in this place for the next three days with nothing to do."

"I thought that's why I came here."

"For you maybe. I'm supposed to be playing tennis."

"So play tennis," Marla told her. "I'll find things to do."

"Like what?"

"Like Mark Lorrington."

Kyla looked skeptically at Marla. "Mark Lorrington?"

"What's the matter with Mark?"

Kyla shook her head. "Nothing, I guess. It's just that, well, nothing he says surprises me," she stated matter-of-factly.

"What's that supposed to mean?"

Kyla shrugged. "He's predictable."

"Maybe some of the other guys in the tennis clinic won't be so predictable when they get here tomorrow."

"Is that all you can think about, Marla?" Kyla complained. "How to get a date?"

Marla looked at her best friend. They'd known each other since they were eleven. "Kyla, sometimes I almost think you don't like guys."

"Guys are fine," Kyla said noncommittally. "I like Tyrone. He's smart." She added quickly, "And cute too."

"And boring."

"How can you say that? You don't even know him."

"Trust me," Marla said dismissively.

They had dinner in the Keewatin's enormous restaurant, where wide plate-glass windows overlooked the lawn and the lake. Other than several elderly couples at different tables, the room was virtually deserted. While they ate, a lingering twilight gathered over the grounds, spreading from the shadows of the forest at the edge of the lawn, and thickening the air. Stars began to appear in the sky over the lake. They had barely finished when Mark Lorrington sauntered between the rows of empty tables to where they sat near the window. He wore a red college jacket with white leather sleeves and dark cotton chinos, and he was all smiles.

"I was hoping I'd find you here!" Without giving the girls time to invite him, he pulled up a chair.

"So I guess our tennis clinic's delayed until Monday," Kyla said morosely.

Mark nodded. "You heard how McKenna dislocated his shoulder? Throwing his tennis racquet at a referee. I heard the other guys coming for the clinic have postponed their arrivals until Sunday."

Marla looked stunned. "Great, you mean we're here all alone for the entire weekend?"

Mark flashed a wide smile. "I wouldn't say all alone. For one thing, tomorrow's Friday, and weekend guests will be arriving." He turned to Kyla. "Say, how about a few games tomorrow?"

Kyla brightened. "I'd love to."

Mark plunged on. "You guys want to come down to the lakeshore for a little bonfire tonight? Tyrone's down there now. He's reverted to his Canadian lumberjack origins and he's chopping wood." He looked at Marla, waiting for an answer.

Marla glanced across the table at Kyla. "I dunno," she said, searching her friend's face for some sign of what she wanted. As usual, when it came to guys, Kyla's eyes were blank.

"Think it's safe? Or have they caught Weird Sylvain, the cannibal of Kenora?" Kyla wanted to know.

Mark looked at both girls and blinked his hazel eyes like a puppy dog. "Tyrone and I promise to protect you." He gave them a deliberately phony smile, and arched his eyebrows. When he relaxed and looked at Marla, his handsome, tanned face was an open invitation.

"I could use the fresh air," Marla offered, nudging Kyla under the table with her foot.

Kyla smiled and nodded. "Sure, I'd love to."

They went back to their rooms to change into warmer clothes. With darkness, the air had turned quite cool. Marla caught herself in the bathroom mirror as she slipped on her blue jeans. She stopped and examined her waist. She had eaten too much at dinner. She looked guiltily toward the bathroom door. No one would know, not even Kyla.

Before she knew it she had the tap turned on. She reached for a glass, filled it, drank, filled it again. Three big glasses. She knelt by the toilet and pressed the spot at the back of her tongue.

Afterward there was a moment of relief that vanished almost as soon as it had come. She prodded herself to get up, scooped water into her mouth, and spat it into the sink. Then she sprayed the air with the small bottle of room deodorizer she always carried, and checked herself in the mirror. Already she thought she looked better, more slender, and the intruding weight at her waist was noticeably gone.

Calmly, she continued dressing. She had just finished pulling on a cashmere sweater when there was a loud knock at the door. She expected Kyla, but it was Mark. She let him into her room, and rummaged in her suitcase for a short plaid jacket that was lined and fairly warm. She found it, and put it on in front of the mirror. Mark stood behind her, eyeing their reflections in the glass as she pulled her long brown hair out from under the jacket's collar.

"So what do you do in New York?" He was standing very close.

"I go to school," Marla said slowly. "I model." She could feel warmth from his body, and felt frozen, unable to move.

"You look like a model," Mark said after a long pause. He moved perceptibly closer, and she was aware of his breathing.

A loud rap sounded at the door, startling them both.

It opened and Kyla popped in. She was surprised to see Mark there. "You guys ready?"

Mark looked disappointed. Marla slipped away from him and grabbed some leather gloves on the bedside table. She took a deep breath. "Ready."

CHAPTER 6

Outside the old hotel it was even cooler than the girls had anticipated. Kyla shivered, and felt her nose grow cold in the icy air. She could almost see a light halo of steam when she breathed. Mark led them across the lawn to the edge of the lake, where a long wooden pier jutted out into the water. They turned, passed through a glade of white-barked birch trees, and entered the forest. The air was redolent with the fragrance of pine. The lights of a small campfire flickered in a clearing, where smooth gray rocks fronted the shore. Across the lake the lights of Kenora glittered softly, and then trailed out to complete and total darkness, where the great northern forest began.

Tyrone stood up from the fire and greeted them when they entered the clearing. He was wearing a red plaid jacket, jeans, and scuffed ankle-high workboots. He did look like a lumberjack.

"Do you live at the Keewatin too?" Marla asked.

"We have a cabin two minutes down the lake from here. We rent it from the hotel." He pointed at the sky. "When was the last time you saw stars like that?"

Marla looked up and gasped. The sky was almost white. The great spiral arms of the Milky Way swirled in vast arcs from horizon to horizon. She'd never seen so many burning so brightly.

"No cities," said Tyrone softly, watching her. Marla looked at him curiously. "There are no cities around here," he repeated. "Just forest all the way to the North Pole. Winnipeg is more than two hundred miles away, and Thunder Bay is three hundred. So you can really see the stars here at night. Not like L.A. The city lights are so bright, they pretty much drown out the starlight."

"And the smog's too thick," Mark added.

Tyrone pointed to two huge logs set at angles upwind to the fire so the smoke and sparks blew in the opposite direction. They sat.

"How do you know what the stars in L.A. look like?" Marla asked.

"I was an exchange student at Mark's high school for a year."

"Yeah, Tyrone, my old Canuck buddy, came to lala-land for some fun in the sun." Mark sat on the log beside Tyrone. "My dad thinks he's a good influence on me."

"Not!" Tyrone said emphatically, laughing. He poked at the fire with a long stick. "I sure covered your butt a few times though," he said, only half joking.

Mark looked at Kyla and Marla. "In Santa Monica, parties rule, and if you can't party hearty, you don't cut it." He snickered, but there was a scornful tone to it. "Tyrone was my designated driver."

Kyla leaned toward Marla and whispered quietly, "Predictable?" Marla shot her an exasperated look.

Tyrone silently reached forward to stir the fire again, reflecting on the year in Los Angeles. It hadn't been just a matter of getting Mark home from parties after he'd passed out. It was helping Mark cover it up from his father. Inevitably, Tyrone became implicated in Mark's duplicity, and he hadn't liked it one bit.

Marla moved closer to the fire, holding her hands out to feel its heat. The flames cast a golden glow across her face. She gazed through a frame of twin pines that stood together on the lakeshore. Farther away, Kenora's lights gleamed upon the water. "This place is too beautiful to have a curse on it," she reflected.

Suddenly Mark sprang to his feet and hunched before the fire, his face distorted. He used his fingers to form antlers at the side of his head. He danced back and forth, incanting in a terrible voice:

> *Its lips are hungry blubbery,*
> *And smacky,*
> *Sucky,*
> *Rubbery!*
> *The wendigo!*
> *The wendigo!*
> *I saw it just a friend ago!*

Tyrone shifted uncomfortably on the log until Mark finished. "Some poem we had to learn in grade school," he laughed, walking back to his log.

"Wendigos sound sort of like a native people's version of a wolf man," Kyla suggested.

"They're much more dangerous," Tyrone explained.

"For one thing, they're shape-shifters. They can grow or shrink in size at will, even disguise themselves by changing into their human form. And they paralyze you or make themselves invisible through a kind of instant hypnosis. Their voices can be as loud as a train whistle, or just a whisper in your ear."

"I've known guys like that," Marla laughed, speaking sideways to Kyla.

The fire crackled, and some of the burning logs fell in.

Mark, who had been staring intently at the fire, looked up and began to speak quietly. "If you listen carefully at night, you can hear their victims as they fly overhead, shouting, 'Oh, my feet of fire—'"

"'My burning feet of fire,'" Tyrone echoed in a drawn-out, haunted voice. His eyes met Mark's, and they laughed. Tyrone looked at the girls. "It's from another story."

"Scariest thing in my life when I was a kid," Mark admitted.

"Anything else we should know?" Kyla asked. "Just in case I bump into one of them while I'm up here in the woods."

"An entire race of them is reputed to live on an island in Hudson Bay," Mark said. "When the winters are really long and cold they come south, looking for new victims."

"What about that one your mom mentioned?" Marla asked.

"Willie Beaver." Tyrone nodded. "He was a trapper who came back to the reservation after eight months in the forest last year. He seemed perfectly normal, but the next morning he was calmly sitting in front of his house, covered with blood. During the night he'd slaughtered his family and started eating them."

Kyla shuddered. "I hope he's in jail."

"Actually, he got away," said Mark. He looked at Tyrone. "Or have the Mounties caught him yet?"

Tyrone shook his head. "And I don't think they will either. According to native custom, if you're possessed by the wendigo, you're supposed to submit willingly to death for the good of the tribe. I think Willie Beaver turned himself in to his own people. I don't think the Mounties will even find a body."

"You guys are making this all up," Marla said doubtfully.

Kyla giggled. "Don't people get enough to eat up here? I mean, between Weird Sylvain and this guy Willie Beaver—"

"That's exactly what it's all about," Tyrone announced. "Starvation. Hundreds of years ago, if the hunting failed, natives starved to death—or survived by eating one another."

Mark looked at Marla and Kyla. "The weak died, and their bodies fed the strong."

"So they created a cannibal monster in their stories and myths," Tyrone continued. "And when it possesses you, it makes you so hungry, everything—or everyone—looks edible."

"So next time you eat a member of your family, blame it on the wendigo," Mark joked.

"Around here, people do," Tyrone insisted.

"The wendigo doesn't—" Kyla started.

"Be careful when you say its name out loud," Tyrone interrupted. He pretended to peer among the dark shadows that spread from the evergreen forest. "All it takes to call one of them is to say the word out loud."

Mark snickered derisively and stood up. He threw his head back and shouted as loudly as he could. "Wen-di-gooooo! Wendigoooo!" His calls were followed by a deathly silence, the moan of wind in the pine needles, and then, from the far shore it echoed back, faint and eerie, "Wen-di-goooo! Wendigoooo!"

Marla glanced at Tyrone again and noticed that he seemed troubled. A wind sighed through the pine trees, swinging the heavy lower branches. Suddenly, an outburst of wild, raucous laughter from somewhere near the lake startled her. Marla jumped, her heart leaping into her throat. The laughter was followed by the sound of splashing water.

Kyla gripped Marla's shoulder and stood up. "What was that?"

"Loons!" Tyrone laughed.

"Those black and white checkered swans on the sign of your mom's shop," Marla exclaimed. She laughed. "Gracious loons."

The mad laughter sounded again, cackles followed by loud, clownlike whoops. It was infectious. Everyone was smiling.

"Loons are never gracious, really," Tyrone muttered.

"I'm going down to the lake to see them," Kyla announced. "Any takers?"

Tyrone volunteered. Mark and Marla were left alone by the fire. It was burning low, the logs crumbling to powdery white ash and hot coals glowing orange against the night.

Mark stood and walked over to the log where Marla sat. She moved over to give him room.

"I didn't figure on meeting a beautiful babe on this trip to the Keewatin," he said lightly.

Marla waited a moment before answering. She didn't

like being called a babe. "I bet come summer, the Keewatin's a regular babefest."

Mark looked at her curiously, surprised by her scarcely veiled sarcasm. "I get what I want," he said slowly. "What about you? Do you get what you want?"

Marla paused. "Sometimes," she answered reluctantly, not quite sure what she meant. She decided to change the subject. "So you're planning on going pro?" she asked, referring to Mark's tennis ambitions.

"It was that or a rock star," Mark answered confidently and without a trace of irony.

"And what if tennis doesn't work out?" Marla asked.

"It's all out there," Mark told her. "You just gotta take it. I'm going to be famous someday. I already know that much. It's just a question of how."

"What's so important about being famous?" It was a question Marla had asked a lot after she started appearing on the covers of magazines. And she'd yet to hear an answer that satisfied her.

"You're born, you live, you die," Mark said. "What's the point of it all if you don't leave your mark?"

"I dunno. Maybe I still have to figure out how to live before I start worrying about being dead." Marla thought about how her face, her body, her smile, were adored by photographers and magazine editors, but her looks were just a genetic accident. They didn't make her feel any better about who she was inside.

"So you're a model," Mark said. "Say, you looked kind of familiar when I first met you. Are you in magazines?"

Marla smiled graciously. It was a practiced smile. "I've even done a few covers."

"So you're already famous." There was a look in

Mark's eyes, somewhere between admiration and resentment.

"Well, I guess my face is. Problem with being famous is that people think you have it all even if you don't."

"That's the whole point!" Mark said excitedly, as if Marla had just proved something for him. "It doesn't matter what the truth is—only what people *think* it is."

Marla struggled for a response. She was certain that what Mark was saying was all wrong. Silence fell between them. They saw Kyla and Tyrone walking up from the lakeshore, talking animatedly.

"Guess if I walk you home, I have to walk your girlfriend home too," Mark said.

It was a proposition. Marla decided to decline it.

"Guess so." She stood, turning to watch Kyla and Tyrone approach the circle of light put off by the glowing coals of the fire. A strong, cold wind pushed its way across the clearing, blowing ashes and sparks from the fire and rattling the branches of the pine trees.

"Ready to go back?" Kyla suggested, stepping into the clearing around the fire.

Marla nodded silently. The wind was as cold as ice, and despite her jacket, she shivered. Tyrone doused the bonfire with a container of water and stirred the soggy embers until he was certain it was out.

Marla glanced overhead at the stars one last time before heading back to the hotel. Far overhead, something high in the northern sky orbited smoothly, blotting out the stars as it raced to the edge of the horizon. She shivered again, but this time it wasn't the sudden cold. It was that strange, inexplicable feeling she'd had in the city a few days earlier.

She felt like she was being watched.

* * *

The four teenagers walked back to the Keewatin together. Tyrone parted company first, walking down a trail that led behind the Keewatin to his cabin. Inside the hotel, Marla and Kyla took the elevator to their third-floor rooms.

Mark went to his family's private suite, a spacious apartment that commanded a magnificent view of Lake of the Woods, and the lights of Kenora twinkling along the shore. As he undressed, he plotted a strategy of seduction.

Marla, after all, was a major fox. Her friend Kyla was an ice queen. He could have either of them, he thought, picking up his tennis racquet. Getting girls had always been easy for him, and he took it for granted that he got what he wanted.

He played air tennis for a minute, swinging his racquet and watching his reflection in the mirror. He was determined to be a champion tennis player whether his father or anyone else liked it or not.

Since he was ten years old Mark had been going to tennis camps. He was good, but it was no secret that his father's money had bought him a place on the southern California tennis circuit, not real talent. And as the owner of the Keewatin, his father had gotten him a place in Tom McKenna's clinic.

McKenna was Mark's hero. He ruled the courts. And when McKenna had a tantrum and threw a racquet at a referee, Mark thought it was cool. No one told McKenna what to do, because he was a champion. And that's what Mark dreamed of. Being a champ meant having power—and power was what Mark Lorrington wanted.

He lay back against his pillow, his head filled with

images of tennis courts, the sound of a huge audience roaring acclaim, his arms over his head in the posture of victory, reporters shoving microphones and cameras in his face, awaiting his words. After that would be endorsements, television commercials, maybe even a line of tennis equipment with his signature on every item. Mark fell asleep, visions of glory still dancing in his head.

Hours later Mark awoke abruptly. The room was freezing cold. He glanced around. The night was silent. A cold silver light billowed in the open window. For a moment he thought snowflakes danced in the moonbeams. He shivered, and jumped out of bed.

The smooth wooden floor was ice cold. He walked to the window and was about to shut it, when he noticed a clump of ragged green moss hanging from the brass clasp that locked the windows. Outside, the grounds of the hotel swam in the luminous glow from a moon that floated like a silver coin, radiant, and just past full.

Something made Mark look down. His feet were floating above the floor. Suddenly he felt as if he were being sucked through the window. He'd never felt so cold. He was flying over the lake at tremendous speed, then over the primeval Canadian forest, where millions of fir trees stretched across the earth below him as far as he could see, broken by patches of weathered rock, swamps, and the dark, shiny surfaces of hundreds of lakes. He was traveling at an incredible speed, until the landscape below was almost a blur, an unending vista of rock, tree, lake, rock, tree, lake, the sound of the wind like a pitching scream in his ears.

He blinked against the icy wind that froze his eyes, and wriggled his fingers and toes against the cold. Suddenly, strangely, warmth flooded his body. He was aware of the cold, yet somehow could not feel it. His stomach growled. His mouth filled with saliva. And deep in his gut he began to feel a hunger more ravenous than any he had ever known.

CHAPTER 7

Marla slept late Friday morning. The sun was bright and warm when she got up, so she put on a two-piece bathing suit under blue jeans and a cotton blouse. Kyla was already gone from her room. Marla skipped breakfast, settling instead for a can of juice from a vending machine.

It was almost eleven when she arrived at the terrace overlooking the lake, where rows of white metal chaise longues waited for summer sunbathers. She was loaded down with magazines to read, and hope eternal, a bottle of tanning lotion. The sky was blue and cloudless. The sun beamed like a golden eye across the dappled surface of the lake. The long boughs of enormous pine trees surrounding the terrace swayed lightly in warm spring breezes. Marla breathed deeply. The air smelled sweet and green.

The terrace was virtually empty except for an elderly couple who sat at a table on the other side, warming themselves in the sun and not saying a word to each other. As Marla stretched her leg over a chaise and fell back in it, she wondered if that's what happened to couples that were together for too long—by the time they grew old they no longer had anything to say to each other. She couldn't remember her own mother and father ever having a real conversation together. They seemed to inhabit separate universes. Mrs. Drake had been so busy launching Marla's career as a child actress, perhaps it was no wonder her father had looked for attention elsewhere.

Marla kicked back her jeans and reached for the sunscreen, when a shadow fell across her, blocking the sun. She turned around and saw Kyla standing beside the chaise, wearing her tennis whites and holding her racquet. Her blond hair was damp with sweat.

Kyla put her hand out as if feeling for rain. "I feel the sun," she said matter-of-factly. "But barely. Don't waste your suntan lotion."

"Are you kidding," Marla said, pumping a small lake of creamy goo into the palm of her hand and smearing it down her long, slender legs. "It has sunscreen in it. You realize, of course, that the ozone layer is totally gone over this part of the northern hemisphere."

Mark Lorrington loped energetically up the steps from the lawn to the terrace. He was wearing dark sunglasses, and a light blue nylon jacket over his tennis whites. When he saw them, he grinned and walked over.

"What happened to that California tan?" Marla asked casually, noting that it seemed to have disappeared overnight.

Mark shrugged, ignoring the question, and looked at Kyla. "Did you fill Marla in on the plans?"

"Not yet."

Mark turned to Marla. "Tyrone and I want to go hiking this afternoon. You're invited."

"Since there's nothing else to do, I thought you might be interested," Kyla offered.

"Sounds great." Marla nodded. "You want to join Kyla and me for lunch first?"

Mark shook his head. "Uh, I'll grab something on my own," he answered quickly. "Look, I gotta run. See you guys out front at one." He waved with his tennis racquet and crossed the terrace.

"Was he out partying last night?" Marla asked Kyla quietly. "He's so pale, he looks like death warmed over."

"Sure doesn't play like he's hung over. In fact, he beat me every game but one."

Marla looked at Kyla with surprise. "That's a little weird, isn't it? How come he's so good?"

Kyla shook her head. "His form is lousy, but he moves. Every time I sank the ball in his far court, he'd suddenly be right there, knocking it back." She paused a moment, watching Mark disappear inside the French doors to the hotel. "He's fast. Unbelievably fast."

Mark was sitting at the wheel of a Jeep when Marla and Kyla walked out the front doors of the Keewatin at one o'clock. Tyrone was in the passenger seat. His eyes lit up when he saw Marla. He stepped down and held the door open.

"Take the front seat," he offered. "You'll see more."

"We're going on some rough gravel roads, so I took this four-wheel-drive from the hotel car pool," Mark explained. Kyla sat in the backseat, and Tyrone climbed in beside her.

"Where are we going, exactly?" Marla asked as Mark pulled out of the circular drive and onto the road.

"There're some hiking trails up to a beautiful waterfall," Tyrone explained.

Mark drove onto the main highway and headed west, back toward the tiny Kenora airport. Three miles past the airport he turned onto another paved road, a two-lane blacktop that led straight through the forest, as if a razor had slashed across the face of the earth. Densely packed spruce trees, their branches wild and tangled, pressed against the broad ditches that lined each side of the road. They were half-filled with muddy brown water and cattails. Red-winged blackbirds flickered among the tall grasses. Mark drove for almost an hour and there was little change of scenery.

"This forest goes on forever," Marla announced finally.

Tyrone leaned forward from the backseat. "For thousands of miles."

"It's almost too wild. As if people don't really belong here."

"They don't," Mark interjected, speaking loudly over the sound of the engine. "They belong in places like Santa Monica and New York City." He gestured with his head at Tyrone in the backseat. "Except for rubes like this dude."

Tyrone ignored the comment. "These rocks are a billion years old. It's the oldest landscape on the planet."

"It feels old," Marla said. "Sort of spooky too. I have no idea why."

"Because it's hostile to human life," Tyrone stated flatly. "I mean, it looks like a vacation wonderland, but the wilderness will kill you. If you get lost, you die. From starvation. Or exposure."

"Or wild animals?" Marla wondered out loud.

Tyrone laughed. "Not unless you get between a mother bear and her cubs. No, the animals aren't very dangerous here. But—" He stopped, and stared out the window at the passing trees, apparently unwilling to say anything more.

"But what?" Kyla prodded.

Tyrone was quiet a moment. "When we're kids we're brought up on fairy tales like 'Hansel and Gretel,' you know, where they go into the woods and find a gingerbread house and defeat the witch and on the other side of the forest they find another village and safety. Here there is no other side of the forest. It just goes on and on, until it reaches the Arctic Ocean. Empty." He paused again. "And no gingerbread houses either. Nothing human."

Marla turned around to look at him. "Meaning?"

Tyrone opened his mouth to say something, and once again seemed to think better of it.

"Well," Marla prodded him.

Tyrone took a deep breath. "Look, I'm not saying it is or it isn't, but settlers and fur traders have been here what, two, three hundred years tops. Native people have been here for thirty or forty thousand years. They have all kinds of stories about creatures who live in the forests. Giants and little people. Tree and animal spirits."

"So what are you saying?" Kyla demanded. "These spirits exist?"

Tyrone gave an exaggerated shrug. "Maybe native people see things that people from Europe don't. Maybe they've just been here long enough to know the forest better than we do. Or maybe if a lot of people believe in something, it starts to exist."

"Like the wendigo?" Marla suggested, rolling her eyes. Frankly, she'd heard enough about cannibal monsters.

"We're almost there," Mark announced loudly, braking the Jeep. He turned onto a one-lane gravel road that led straight into the forest. He drove another fifty yards, the Jeep bouncing and tilting precariously over deep potholes in the rutted gravel. The road ended abruptly in a small clearing. Mark brought the Jeep to a halt, and turned off the ignition.

When the engine died, Marla was instantly aware of the forest's great silence, an absence unfilled by the buzz of civilization. As she opened her door and stepped down from the Jeep, she listened to the others, the Jeep's doors opening and shutting, Tyrone and Mark hauling their knapsacks from the back, Kyla's running shoes crunching on the gravel as she approached the edge of the forest, even the barely audible whisper of a breeze filtering through the surrounding forest. But behind all that there was only an immense, unbroken silence.

"I hear water!" Kyla shouted. She stepped beyond the first row of trees. Despite the sunlight in the clearing, the forest's dark shadows almost completely obscured her.

Tyrone pulled up beside Marla, slinging a knapsack over his shoulder. He gestured at Mark, who was slamming the back door of the Jeep closed. "Our benefactor got the Keewatin's kitchen to pack some sandwiches and sodas."

Mark came around the side of the vehicle carrying a second knapsack. As he reached his arms through the straps, his sunglasses flew to the ground and landed next to Marla. She knelt and retrieved them.

"You won't really need these in the woods," she said, offering them to him.

Mark snatched his sunglasses from her outstretched hand. "Thanks." His eyes were seriously bloodshot. He put them on. "Sun's still pretty bright," he added quickly. He followed Kyla into the woods.

"Ready?" Tyrone asked, walking over to Marla. He had been solicitous to her all afternoon.

"What's with the dude in the sunglasses," Marla asked quietly, watching Mark disappear between the first row of trees. "His future's so bright he's gotta wear shades?"

"Lorrington has a pretty high opinion of himself," Tyrone answered evasively. "And he likes to be the center of attention. But he's decent. Really."

"You're very loyal," Marla observed.

Tyrone made a face. "Mark and I grew up together, every summer since we were little kids. I guess he's my best friend."

They walked into the forest, a sudden coolness falling across their skin, and the smell of verdure pervading the air. Ahead of them, they heard babbling water. Kyla and Mark were standing on gray rocks at the edge of a shallow stream. The water was crystal-clear, flowing over stones and gravel. The bank on the other side was smooth gray rock sloping upward to a tangled forest of fir and birch.

Kyla knelt and dipped her hand in the water. "Ouch!" She quickly withdrew it. "Icy." She shook the water off and dried her hand on her jeans.

Tyrone laughed. "There's still snow and ice in the forest."

"In May?" Marla said, incredulous. She looked around. Sunlight filled the opening in the forest where the stream meandered. The birch tree's leaves had barely unfurled, and were like halos of light green glowing from white-barked branches. But the ground was dry, and there was no evidence of winter.

"Sure." Tyrone smiled. "Wait. I'll show you."

He led them to a trail that ran along the edge of the little stream. At times it detoured into the forest, around brambles, massive fallen trees, or outcroppings of ancient stone, but always they heard the stream burbling on their right. They came abruptly to a place where the forest ended at a ledge, and the land gave way, exposing a great valley of evergreens spotted with tiny lakes that sparkled under the afternoon sun. The four teenagers stopped and gazed.

Marla walked close to the edge, aware of a breeze blowing up from the valley, tugging at her hair. It was warm from the sun, but a faint iciness from the forest floor lingered beneath the warmth. There was something ancient about the vast landscape. It was immense with time.

"I feel like it's kind of alive," said Marla after a while. "As though the rocks and hills are only sleeping."

Tyrone laughed. "And once every million years or so they wake up, breathe, look around to check out the action, and fall back asleep for another eon."

"It's bigger than us," said Kyla softly.

Mark stood near the edge of the forest in the shadow of a twisted pine tree. "Listen to you guys," he called to them. "It's just rocks and trees. More nature for man to conquer."

"I dunno about that," Tyrone murmured, still gazing over the northern landscape. From the corner of his eye he caught Marla looking at him strangely, and smiled at her.

"C'mon, let's get out of here," Mark shouted impatiently.

Marla, Kyla, and Tyrone walked back toward the stream, with Mark leading the way.

"I think I know what you mean about this forest belonging to the Indians, not to settlers," Kyla remarked to Tyrone.

"Native people," Tyrone corrected her.

Kyla nodded. "Native people. All those European fairy tales about werewolves and trolls, witches and gingerbread houses—none of them fits here. The land is too wild."

"How do you kill a wendigo?" Marla asked, wondering why the question popped into her head.

Tyrone looked at her curiously.

"Silver bullets?" Kyla joked.

"Hey, that's an idea!" Tyrone agreed, laughing. Then he shook his head. "You have to melt its heart of ice."

"Hark!" Mark shouted back at them. He had stopped and put his hand in the air to motion silence. Through the densely packed trees Marla heard a distant, steady thunder.

"The waterfall!" Mark yelled. He bounded into the woods, weaving between trees and quickly disappearing.

Marla and Kyla looked at Tyrone, who gestured in the direction Mark had gone. "Straight ahead."

A few seconds later the three of them broke through the forest to a wide clearing, where sun-baked rocks, cracked from winters of frost and smooth from centuries of wind, spread away from a stone basin. A single torrent of water fell almost thirty feet from the top of a cliff of black rock.

They descended to the water. Fir trees pressed

against the rock, and the sun was already far enough beyond the top of the cliff to throw the pool into shadow for the rest of the day. The air was noticeably cooler. Water had percolated through crevasses lining the ancient black rock, and a giant column of ice grew from the side of the cliff.

"Awesome," Kyla said.

"The sun's still not high enough at this time of year to give this more than an hour of light a day," Tyrone explained. "It'll take another month to melt that." He swung his knapsack off his back, unzipped it, and reached inside for a soda. "Anyone need ice?" he asked with a laugh.

Marla looked down at the swaths of bright green moss growing along the contours of the stone. The soft vegetation had been crushed by an enormous circular footprint with a single great toe. "Omigod!" she murmured quietly.

The others looked at her, and she pointed to the moss at her feet.

"It's a wendigo footprint!" Mark said lightly.

Marla began to tremble. She had seen a footprint like that before—in the thin wet snow on a sidewalk in New York. The night she had been followed!

CHAPTER 8

"Get real, Mark," Kyla said dismissively. "It's only a story." She looked at Tyrone for confirmation.

"Sure," he said, kneeling to look at the mark in the moss. "Some animal took a nap here. A porcupine or a raccoon."

They unpacked the knapsacks and set out the lunch of carefully boxed sandwiches from the Keewatin's kitchen. Marla was suddenly intensely hungry—she'd gone to lunch with Kyla earlier, but had picked at her food and eaten almost nothing. The long ride and the fresh air made her ravenous. Now, she noticed, it was Mark who was picking at his food. He put a half-eaten sandwich back into a box and stood.

"I'm going to take a walk," he announced. "Meet you guys back here in a while." Without waiting for anyone to respond, he started walking back down the stream.

"What's up above the falls?" Kyla asked when he was gone.

"Red Hawk Lake," said Tyrone. "There's a trail up there."

"Uphill?" Marla asked, crinkling her nose. "I was thinking about a nap. Lying on a hot rock and soaking up sun."

"It'll take only ten minutes," Tyrone said.

"Let's do it," Kyla urged.

Marla hesitated. "What about Mark?"

"You heard him," Tyrone said. "He'll meet us back here."

Tyrone filled one of the knapsacks with sodas, and they left the other one by the pond. The trail to Red Hawk Lake, much to Marla's surprise, was easy. Farther along the black rock the slope became gentle, and a trail of packed earth wound back and forth along a cliff. As they climbed, the view of the rolling carpet of fir trees that spread out below grew more and more spectacular.

Marla and Kyla were huffing and puffing by the time the ground leveled off again. Fir trees were gone, replaced by a forest of tall, thin poplars crowned with heads of small green leaves. There was little undergrowth, making their passage easy. Suddenly they were standing on the edge of a long, narrow lake. Water lapped against the rocks on the shore.

Tyrone pointed to a marsh that spread across the end of the lake not far away. "That's where the lake drains into the waterfall and stream below."

"There's a canoe out there!" Marla cried excitedly. She could make out the characteristic curved end on the far side. The rest was hidden by bulrushes.

"It's probably from the Ojibway reservation way down the lake."

The canoe glided from the marsh. An old man and a

boy were sitting in it, both paddling. They steered the canoe along the shore. The old man, who sat in the bow, spotted the teenagers. He motioned to the boy in the stern. The canoe changed direction and approached the shore.

Marla could make out their faces as they came closer. The old man's face was lined and weathered to the texture of tree bark from years of sun, wind, and snow. He wore a thick wool jacket of red and black plaid, and his long gray hair was tied back with a faded red bandanna. The boy was barely a teenager, and wore a similar plaid jacket of dark green. His shiny black hair had been clipped at the shoulders.

"Hello!" Tyrone shouted, waving.

The two natives stopped paddling about twenty feet from the shore and let the canoe glide smoothly across the water on its own momentum. They stared impassively at the three teenagers, making no effort to speak or even make a gesture of greeting. Nearby, a red-winged blackbird fluttered nervously atop a cattail.

"That's White Eagle," Tyrone whispered quietly into Marla's ear. "He's a shaman."

"Shaman?"

Tyrone nodded. "Medicine man. A traditional healer. Ethnobotanists from Ottawa came here last year to learn about natural medicines and herbs from him. There was an article in the newspaper about it."

The canoe was only ten feet from shore. The bottom was filled with plump fish, their silvery scales coruscating with sunlight. The boy in the stern stuck his paddle back into the water and ruddered the canoe sideways until it was parallel to the shore, a few feet from the teenagers. In the bow, White Eagle put his hand up in a silent greeting. His eyes were friendly.

Marla gestured to the lake and the forest. "You live in a very beautiful country. I'm visiting here. From New York."

White Eagle smiled broadly. "That is very far away." His voice was deep and sounded younger than he looked. Each word was pronounced clearly and distinctly. He reached back and picked up one of the fish lying in the bottom of the canoe. Holding it aloft with his finger and thumb inserted in the poor beast's gills, he held it over the edge of the canoe, offering it to her. "We have fished well today and have too much now."

"Fresh trout," Tyrone said quietly to Marla. "Take it. The chefs will cook it for you at the Keewatin."

"Ugh," Marla commented. "It's slimy. You take it."

Tyrone chuckled and leaned out over the water, taking the plump trout from White Eagle and holding it the same way, with his fingers inserted in the fish's gills. He shucked off his knapsack, dumped the sodas out of a brown paper bag, and started wrapping the fish.

"Thank you so much," Marla said to the two natives. "We'll cook it at the Keewatin."

Almost instantly, White Eagle's face seemed to visibly darken, and his bushy white brows flickered. "The great hotel is cursed," he said, looking away.

Marla heard someone passing heavily through the underbrush.

"It's Mark," Kyla said, standing beside Marla.

Mark Lorrington stepped from the forest of birch trees onto the rocks along the lakeshore. He stopped when he saw the canoe, and made no attempt to come closer.

White Eagle's face grew darker. He turned around to face the boy in the stern and spoke rapidly in his native language. The boy dipped his paddle into the water, pushing the canoe away from the shore.

Marla looked at White Eagle, but his friendliness was gone. The old man pulled his paddle through the water while the boy ruddered the canoe away from the shore.

"Thank you for your gift," Marla called to them.

"We must go," White Eagle said sternly as the canoe drew farther from the shore. "Our hearts are like water." The bow of the canoe swung around. Picking up speed, they headed out into the lake.

"What was that all about, that their hearts are like water," Kyla asked, staring after the canoe.

Tyrone scratched his head. He looked puzzled. "He meant they were afraid," he answered, staring into the distance after them. He looked at the two girls and shrugged.

Mark shouted to them from the edge of the trees. "I found a different trail to go back down." The other three teens walked back and joined him. "I climbed up the cliff on the other side of the waterfall and crossed back over on some stones in the marsh. Come on, I'll show you."

Without waiting for a response, he darted into the woods, leading them toward the marsh. The afternoon sun was getting lower in the west, making the shadows longer. Already a chill had settled over the woods, draining the warmth from the last remnants of sunlight.

The marsh ended at a rock-filled stream, where the water ran faster, splashing and swirling as it coursed toward the waterfall. Stepping stones were strewn through the rushing water, and the teenagers picked their way gingerly to the other side.

"This way," Mark said again. He led them from the precipice of black rock overlooking the waterfall and into a thick pine forest. The trail led down to a wide cleft that ran between high gray rocks shattered and cracked by eons of age and cold. It was cool there, and ice was visible on the sides of the rock where it was sheltered from the sun by outcroppings. In the altered environment the trees and underbrush had barely budded. The trail narrowed into a thin path, disappearing sometimes in brambles or under a fallen tree. Although it was only late afternoon, twilight thickened in the ancient ravine.

"Some trail, Lorrington," Tyrone called out. He followed Marla and Kyla, who walked single file, lagging twenty feet behind Mark.

Suddenly the ravine widened, with broad flat rocks coasting downhill to another gorge, fifty feet away. It was barely more than a cleft cut through the time-worn rock of the ancient pre-Cambrian shield. From the edge Mark shouted impatiently, "You guys coming?"

"Aye, aye, sir!" Kyla muttered sarcastically.

"Are you sure you know where you're going?" Tyrone demanded.

"Actually we did get off the trail I found," Mark admitted. "But the waterfall's on the other side of this gorge. Listen."

In the momentary silence they could hear the thunder of water on rock, not too far away. Once again Mark led the way, scrambling down the side of the gorge, braking his descent by holding on to saplings and rocks. The others followed.

The gorge was barely six feet wide, a narrow ravine between dank rocks. The ground squished with water, and the damp, cold air was tainted by the smell of decaying vegetation. Small piles of ice crystals, the remnants of once-huge drifts of snow, remained in nooks and crevasses against the rock. Kyla picked some up and let them fall through her fingers. When Mark saw her, he grabbed a handful.

"Snowball fight!" he crowed, shaping it into a ball.

"I'll pass," Marla said quietly, pushing past him and continuing along the path. Then she saw something that made her freeze in her tracks. She tried to speak, to call to the others, but her tongue was unable to form words.

Staring at her through eyes like marble was a dead man, as solid as a block of ice, plunked to his waist in the crystalline snow as if he had fallen from the sky, his open mouth frozen in a cry of naked horror.

CHAPTER 9

Marla was aware of Tyrone and Kyla approaching behind her. Kyla stifled a gasp.

"It's Sylvain!" Tyrone said in a hoarse whisper. He put his arms around both Marla and Kyla, pulling them away from the macabre sight.

Mark joined them and stared at the body. "Weird Sylvain," he said slowly, "and *weird* is not the word for it."

Tyrone took charge. They left the body where they found it, and he led them to the waterfall by following the heavy thunder of its waters. There they found the path to where the Jeep was parked. Tyrone phoned the RCMP from a highway gas station, and they returned to the Keewatin, while Mounties went to retrieve the frozen corpse.

A wind came up, blowing in hard from the northwest, driving a bank of slate-gray clouds before it. By evening the sky was overcast, by night it was starless, and pressed against the windows of the Keewatin's dining room. After a pointless dinner at which no one ate—although Mark insisted the meal was on the Keewatin—a Royal Canadian Mounted Police cruiser pulled up to the hotel and two officers emerged.

Constable Robichaud was young and dark-haired, and sported a short, clipped mustache. The other one, Sergeant Clarkson, was middle-aged, his sandy hair graying, and his faced lined. Mark led them to his family's suite. The teenagers sat on two plush, old-fashioned couches that faced each other before a brick fireplace. The pine floors were carpeted with thick red rugs.

The Mounties each took a chair. Robichaud took out a thick notepad and began to write down the teenagers' names and home addresses. Clarkson's sharp blue eyes glanced from Marla to Kyla, then to Tyrone and Mark, studying each of them carefully.

"That was Sylvain all right," Robichaud told them. "After committing murder, he apparently fled into the forest to avoid apprehension."

"He was frozen solid," Tyrone pointed out. "How did he freeze solid at this time of year?"

"He was dead from exposure," Robichaud said in such a tone as to leave no doubt.

"The nights are still cold in the woods," Sergeant Clarkson said. "And that ravine where you found him doesn't get much sunlight."

Tyrone looked at Marla and Kyla, who sat on the couch opposite him. Coolly, he told them, "The wendigo drops its victims from the sky when it's finished with them. At that point the victims are frozen solid from their flight through the high altitude and the wendigo's speed."

"Oh, stop it, Tyrone," Marla snapped suddenly. "You sound like some kind of Dr. Frankenfurter or something."

Constable Robichaud cast a concerned glance in Sergeant Clarkson's direction. "Not another one," he said in an exasperated tone. He looked at Tyrone as if he were a wise guy. "We get enough of that kind of superstitious crap from the natives, who are scared of just about anything that goes bump in the night." He slapped his notepad closed, and added derisively, "Unless it contains alcohol."

Tyrone's eyes suddenly clouded. "I'm sorry I made you uncomfortable," he said, ignoring Robichaud and looking steadily at Marla.

Sergeant Clarkson jumped into the fray. "Look, everyone in town has heard stories that Sylvain had seen the wendigo, as they call it. Sylvain was alcoholic. He heard it so much, he ended up believing it himself. He killed a couple of skid row bums at his cabin, mutilated their bodies, and fled into the woods."

He paused and looked at the teenagers. "This kind of thing happens every now and then—someone turns into a cannibal and starts killing people. The government's even had scientists study it. It's a kind of madness—insanity—that native people suffer, just like white people become paranoids or schizophrenics. No one knows why exactly, even though there are records of wendigo madness that go back four hundred years to the earliest explorers in this part of the country. But it's a pretty big leap of the imagination to say that wendigos actually exist."

"That Willie Beaver case last year, now, that was classic wendigo madness," Constable Robichaud interjected. "Beaver was a trapper and came back to the reservation after eight months on his trap lines. Witnesses say he was a little depressed and moody, but other than that he seemed perfectly normal. During the night he killed his wife and kids and started eating them. He disappeared and we're still looking for him."

"And, like Sylvain, he's probably dead from exposure in the forest," Clarkson concluded. "We'll be lucky if we even find his bones."

"Eaten by animals. *Not* wendigos," Robichaud added emphatically.

The two RCMP officers left. When Kyla and Tyrone stood to leave, Marla lingered. She was restless and not eager to return to her room. She pulled her feet up and nestled in the corner of the big overstuffed couch.

"I'm going home, Kyla," Marla announced suddenly. "Tomorrow. This is not why I got out of New York. If I want to stumble across dead bodies, I'd rather do it in Central Park."

Kyla flopped down on the couch again. "Tomorrow's Saturday. If Tom McKenna doesn't show up on Monday for the tennis clinic, I'll go back with you. Can't you wait until then?"

Tyrone was hovering nearby. "Give it another day," he said to Marla. "It's not like bodies turn up all the time here." Something in his voice seemed urgent, almost pleading, and Marla knew exactly what it was.

"You haven't helped matters any," she snapped at him, suddenly hostile. "You believe all this wendigo stuff, don't you?" She saw Tyrone flinch, and her anger bubbled out, uncontrollable. "You do! You really do!" she taunted. She was aware of Mark, leaning against the fireplace, listening carefully while a mocking smile spread across his face.

"Why don't you just call one, Tyrone," she persisted.

"Call a wendigo and prove to us it really exists!" She pushed herself up and ran to one of the windows overlooking the lake. She threw up the sash. A gust of cold wind leapt into the room. The long white curtains writhed like wraiths. She stuck her head out.

"Wendigoooo!" Marla shouted into the night as loud as she could. She slammed the window shut and turned around to face her friends. "See! It doesn't come."

Tyrone looked at her, his face pale and his eyes dark. "You're right," he said quietly. "I haven't made matters any better. It's just that . . . well, never mind. Good night, everyone."

Without another word he crossed the room and left.

"What do you expect?" Mark snickered. "Tyrone's a rube. He grew up in this hick town. He believes in wendigos."

Marla drooped. Kyla was looking at her, her eyes filled with reproach. "We're all upset," she suggested. "Let's turn in for the night. We can book you a flight in the morning."

Exhausted, Marla returned to her room and prepared for bed. She found herself unable to stop thinking about Tyrone and the way she'd humiliated him. She remembered the hurt look in his eyes. Remorse began to gather in her chest, the worst place, she thought. It meant she was on the verge of tears. Why had she done it, she wondered, and realized she was just pretending not to know the answer.

Tyrone had been nothing but gracious to her almost from the moment she had arrived in Kenora. He was attentive, he opened doors and pulled out chairs for her. When she asked questions about the land, he explained everything so carefully. And every now and then she caught him looking at her with a look in his eyes that had to be—Marla wasn't prepared to call it love, but it was at least an infatuation. An unrequited one, she told herself sternly.

And it scared her. The fact that he was kind, gentle, and considerate, as well as smart, tall, and good-looking made him, by a lot of girls' standards, the perfect boyfriend. Too perfect for me, she thought. She paused before the bathroom mirror and let her robe fall to the floor, smoothing her hands down her thin figure. She'd eaten hardly anything all day again. That was good, she thought. Then Cubbie Cube's cruel words in the New York restaurant taunted her again. "Stuck-up, anorexic . . ."

She could never be intimate with Tyrone. He was too —normal, she thought, fumbling momentarily for the right word—to understand New York and what her life was like there. What she had to do to stay on top as a model. Then that little voice at the back of her mind spoke again with its annoying truth. She put her hands to her ears as if to stop listening to it. It told her she was ashamed of her bulimia. And that she didn't deserve a guy as nice as Tyrone.

That night in bed, Marla dreamed. She knew she was dreaming, although it felt incredibly real, because she was floating a foot above the floor as she crossed her room to the window and pulled it open. A wind entered, icy and somehow solid enough to lift her up and float her outside. She was as light as a feather. She saw the Keewatin below, and began to move quickly through the air.

It was a beautiful dream. She was skimming over the northern wilderness, above hundreds of dark lakes, vast forests of fir trees and long stretches of tundra.

She approached the ragged edge of the land, where it met a great sheet of water strewn with arctic ice floes. The northern lights flickered across the night horizon far ahead of her, and the sky was flecked with stars, glittering like little chunks of ice. Even in her thin nightgown she wasn't cold. She breathed deeply and felt the freezing air nip at her nostrils, sear her lungs. It was invigorating, and, oddly, warmed her. She hovered over the northern landscape, awed by its strange beauty, and aware that she felt good because she had no feelings at all.

She awakened suddenly, her eyes springing open to stare up at the ceiling of her hotel room. Steam was rising above her face, and she realized it was her breath, warm and fogging the air. The room was ice cold. She looked around and saw the window, its sash thrown wide open. That was strange. She had left it open only a crack before turning in. She got out of bed, her bare feet feeling the cold wood floor, and crossed to the window.

The north wind had grown stronger, and the clouds were gone. The night sky was bright with stars. Pine boughs crashed violently against the log sides of the big old hotel, the long, thin needles swirling and undulating in the silver starlight. When she lowered the sash, she noticed moss on the windowsill, and the slightest trace of a strange dank smell.

Marla went back to bed and pulled the covers up. She had felt so secure, so comforted when she was dreaming. Already, she longed to dream again.

Kyla awakened early, as usual, and breakfasted by herself in the Keewatin's cathedrallike restaurant. A

Saturday morning, the hotel was filling up with weekend guests. She'd promised Mark a nine o'clock tennis match, which left her with forty-five minutes. Marla wouldn't be up for hours.

Kyla stopped at the Gracious Loon gift shop for directions. Then she followed a path that led around the back of the Keewatin, past the tennis courts and through a copse of birch trees. The air was crisp and cool, still damp from dew. Ahead of her, a one-story log cabin sat in a clearing. The veranda in front was hung with macramé plant hangers. A great stone chimney testified to an immense fireplace within.

Tyrone was outside, next to a shoulder-high pile of neatly stacked logs. He was wearing a blue plaid shirt with the sleeves rolled up past his biceps. The veins in his arms stood out like cords from the hard work. He set a log upright on a big old stump, raised an ax over his head, and brought it down. The log split neatly in two. He picked up one of the halves and swung again, making quarters. These he threw into a pile on one side. When he reached for another log, he noticed Kyla. Tyrone straightened, dropped the ax, and leaned on it. "How'd you find me?" He smiled.

"Your mom told me how to get here."

"Yeah, the hotel rents the cabin to us." Tyrone lifted the ax and with a broad smile gestured toward the pile of logs. "You've caught me acting out my ancestral pioneering traditions."

"Don't let me stop you." Kyla laughed.

Tyrone picked up a log, set it on the stump, and raised the ax. "Has Marla gone?" he asked. The ax came down, once again cleaving the log neatly in two.

"You like Marla a lot."

"Well, at least someone noticed." Tyrone bent to retrieve the split pieces.

"Marla's noticed," Kyla assured him. "Don't worry about that."

"I guess a country hick like me's a little outclassed by a big-time New York model, eh?" Tyrone quickly split the halves again, and reached for another log.

"Funny," Kyla said.

"What's funny?" Tyrone prodded her.

"I never thought of you as a hick," Kyla said. "You're too smart to be a hick."

"Is that what brings you out here this early? To tell me that?"

"No. I came to talk about Marla."

Tyrone threw the last pieces of split wood aside and stopped chopping. "What about her?"

"Marla needs a break from New York. We should figure out a way to persuade her to stay here for a few more days."

"What's wrong with New York?"

"She knows all the wrong people there."

Kyla saw Tyrone's eyes look past her and focus. "Why don't you just ask her to stay," he suggested.

Kyla turned around. Marla was tripping down the path toward the cabin, bright-eyed and, much to Kyla's astonishment, happy. She was breathing hard from her walk and, although her skin seemed paler than usual, her cheeks were rosy from the fresh air.

"I woke up early," Marla said by way of explanation when she saw the surprise on Kyla's face. "Tyrone's mother said you'd just come down here." She turned to look at Tyrone.

He nodded hello, and waited, smiling shyly.

"I'm sorry about last night, Tyrone," Marla told him.

He set the ax down and took several steps toward her, stripping off his leather work gloves. "No problem." He flashed her a quick smile. "All in all, it was a pretty scary day. But I meant what I said."

"What . . . ?"

"About wanting you to stay a few more days."

"Oh." Marla seemed momentarily taken aback. "Sure." She glanced at Kyla. "At least until you know if Tom McKenna is going to show up on Monday or not."

"Mission accomplished," Tyrone said, looking at Kyla.

When Marla looked puzzled, Kyla glanced at her watch. "Oh, gosh, I have to meet Mark for tennis."

"I'll walk with you," Marla said. Her eyes met Tyrone's.

"See you later," he nodded, returning her smile.

Marla looked back when she and Kyla got to the path. Tyrone was still standing outside the cabin, hands on his hips, watching them leave and, she thought, looking adorable.

"So are you going after Tyrone, Kyla?" she asked, nudging her friend good-humoredly. "Is that what we owe this early morning visit to?"

"Get off," Kyla snorted. There was a pregnant silence between them as they walked up the path toward the Keewatin. "For one thing, he likes you."

Marla sighed as if confronted by a burden.

"He *is* handsome. If you just worked a little harder at being nice to him . . ." Kyla started to suggest. "And stopped obsessing about Mark Lorrington."

"Hey!" Marla stopped her in the middle of the path. "First, I'm definitely not obsessing about Mark. And second, nothing's ruled out, okay? Just let me make up my own mind about it!"

Kyla reached her arm around Marla and squeezed her with a quick hug. "I promise. And I'm glad you're not leaving today."

CHAPTER 10

Marla decided to go into the town of Kenora when Kyla left to play tennis. She asked the desk clerk to call a taxi and had the driver let her out at the lakeshore, near a monument of a gigantic fiberglass and cement fish, four stories high and sculpted as if it were leaping from the waves. Evidently, it was named "Husky the Musky." She walked past it, heading toward the business district.

Kenora was an old town with a few redbrick Victorian buildings scattered among wide swaths of parking lots and modern buildings. Most of these were two stories tall, and rose on a gradual incline that led up from the lakeshore toward the great primeval forest beyond.

On a Saturday morning the town was almost deserted, and Marla saw few people. She walked down a main street to the end of the business district, where rows of small frame houses began. She heard laughter and girls' voices, singing.

*She is beautiful, she is pretty.
She is the queen of the golden city.*

Marla turned a corner onto a side street and saw six native girls skipping rope. They were dressed in their weekend finest, their black hair tied back in pigtails. It was double-Dutch. Two held each end of a long double rope, and a third jumped rapidly in the blur of the swirling ropes. Three looked on, singing in strong voices. It was a skipping song, Marla realized, with a lilting one-two one-two beat that timed the turning of the rope and the skipper's feet. But it was one she had never heard.

*The wind blows strong, the wind blows free,
The wind blows Jo-Ann across the sea.*

Marla watched the girls skip, their smiling eyes like dark shiny stones, and she envied their happiness.

*She is beautiful, she is pretty.
She is the queen of the golden city.*

The words almost seemed to taunt Marla, queen of the golden city, the lucky girl, the model on the cover of magazines, so cool in New York she could hang out with rap stars if she wanted to and how ten thousand—ten million—girls her age would kill to have a life like hers.

The native girls sang faster and the rope turners swung harder. The skipper skipped until her feet were barely visible. She leapt from between the flying ropes, and a second girl jumped in, her feet picking up where the first girl's left off.

*The wind blows strong. The wind blows free.
The wind blows Marla across the sea.*

Marla was startled. Had she heard her own name called, or was she imagining it?

*She is beautiful, she is pretty.
She is the queen of the golden city.*

In her head Marla heard the persistent voices that stopped her on the street, in the corridors at school, at parties, or on dates. "Aren't you Marla Drake, the model?" In their eyes they all wanted something from her, as if some of her good luck, like stardust, might rub off on them. But Marla knew, if no one else did, that on a magazine cover she was nothing more than colored ink, ink and a pretty face. It did nothing to fill the personal emptiness she felt inside. As if really there was no Marla, because everything she did was in the hope that somehow it would make her mother happy and her father stay home. She was fed up. But that said, what was there to do with her anger?

She turned away from the skippers just in time to see someone dart around the building cornering the main street. She had been watched! Once again the feeling that struck her was deep and pervasive, unmistakable. She clenched her teeth. This is what she could do with her anger, she vowed, marching to the corner and looking down the street.

No one was in sight. Shops lined the sidewalks, their darkened plate-glass windows like lidless eyes. A handful of cars cruised the street. Marla started walking, slowly taking in the dreary window displays of hardware stores and stationery shops. But she kept alert, and in the reflection of a plate-glass window finally saw who it was.

He was an odd-looking man of indeterminate age, big, and swathed in a priest's black cassock with a wide-brimmed black monseigneur's hat covering his head. A clerical collar was visible around his neck. He was watching her from the corner. Slowly, Marla pivoted in his direction.

In the blink of an eye he slipped out of sight.

She turned and walked farther down the street, this time stopping to gaze in the dusty window of a bridal shop, where the dresses on the mannequins had yellowed with age. He was back. Once again she caught his reflection in the glass. This time Marla simply moved on until she came to an old brick building on the corner. She turned and broke into a run. Twenty feet away, she darted into a doorway.

She waited, fighting to catch her breath and remain perfectly silent. A moment later she heard footsteps. He passed right in front of her, a big man dressed entirely in black. The clerical collar was clearly visible, but his face was hidden under the wide flat brim of his hat.

Marla decided to confront him. She was about to step out of the doorway, when she suddenly froze. She was unable to move, or, at least, she *felt* unable to move. Seemingly oblivious of her, the priest walked on. Marla's heart pounded in her chest. The man disappeared from the view afforded by the narrow doorway. She willed her body to walk to the sidewalk, but it ignored her. After a moment, as if a spell had broken, she stumbled forward. He was already far down the sidewalk.

Now it was Marla's turn to follow.

He led her to a poorer part of the town, where houses and warehouses were mixed together and storefronts were boarded up. Three native men lolled on the sidewalk, inebriated, barely able to walk, but tightly clutching bottles in paper bags. In a doorway, another native lay almost unconscious and covered in blood from an ugly head wound. His eyes opened, and he gazed up, dazed and passive as she passed. She went past a couple of cheap old hotels sandwiched between a spruced up Salvation Army building. The man she was following disappeared into a doorway.

She approached cautiously, a decaying storefront where the windows had been whitewashed on the inside. A hand-lettered sign hung above the doorway. HOLY MISSION OF ST. FRANCIS. She pushed the battered door, and it swung easily open.

She was standing in a large open space, where gloom filtered through the whitewashed windows. The ceiling was a maze of pipes and sprinklers. Paint peeled from the walls. Around her, tattered couches and battered old coffee tables formed a waiting area. There were several rows of tables opposite a part of the wall where a movable partition had been pulled down over a kitchen counter. Farther on, several rows of metal folding chairs faced a small stage. On it were a pulpit, and a table set with tarnished vessels for Holy Communion.

Like the dream of flying she'd had the night before, she felt afraid, but a strange expectation drew her farther into the room. On a nearby coffee table was a fresh copy of Kenora's Saturday newspaper. The headline read *Fugitive Found Dead.* A paragraph was circled. She peered. It was about the three teenaged tourists and a local boy who had made the bizarre discovery of a frozen corpse in the forest, believed to be that of one

Sylvain Charbadeau. Beside it she saw her face, staring up at her from a torn and dog-eared copy of *Cheeky* magazine.

"I wanted to warn you."

Marla froze, a chill shiver gripping the back of her skull. The voice behind her was almost a growl. She turned slowly, terrified but compelled.

He was standing by the door that led to the kitchen, wearing his flowing black cassock. The hat was gone, revealing a head crowned by gray hair and bushy eyebrows that almost covered his forehead. He towered above her, yet his head was small and round, like a ball perched neatly on his clerical collar. And although his gray hair made him look old, his pale skin was smooth, stretched tightly across his cheekbones and forehead, and strangely scarred around the mouth.

He glanced downward diffidently, not letting Marla look him straight in the eye. He turned abruptly away and stood with his back partly to her.

"But I have been afraid to approach," he said quietly, forcing each word slowly. His voice was smoother but still gruff. He put his hands behind his back and stooped slightly. "I read about the young people who found . . . the body. And this morning I saw you walking, and recognized you." He turned slightly toward Marla and gestured to her face on the cover of the magazine. "People donate magazines to the mission . . ."

Marla stared at him for a moment. "Warn me? About what?" she demanded. Her voice turned accusatory. "You were following me!"

He strode farther into the room and stepped into a shadow before turning to face her. "Perhaps warn is the wrong word. I am Father Francis. My mission is the poor." He spread his arms out in a gesture that encompassed the whole room. "Alcoholics, and the homeless. Many of them are native people."

"Warn me about what?" Marla demanded sharply. Suddenly fearless, she stepped closer, watching the eccentric priest carefully. Something about the man seemed oddly familiar. She remembered the strange figure she'd dreamed of the night before she left New York, precious gemstones cascading through open fingers onto the floor of a windswept tower room. And her dream last night, flying over the great northern landscape, deliciously at peace. She had been alone, and yet, with all the certainty that dreams have, she knew this strange old priest had been there too. The answer to her puzzlement began to form in her head, but the shape of it was far too terrible to acknowledge.

Suddenly a small bat shot across the room, its tiny wings swooping. Marla shrieked and ducked her head, wrapping her hands around her long brown hair. It flew erratically, dipping in circles, and settled on a pipe that crossed the ceiling, hanging upside down. Marla came up for air and eyed the creature warily.

Father Francis was smiling with his scarred, misshapen lips. "Do not be afraid. It is a pet."

He reached inside the folds of his cassock, pulled his hand out, and opened it. Another small furry bat lay in his hand. Flexing its thin black membrane wings, its tiny mouth opened and shut, revealing jagged rows of serrated, needle-sharp teeth.

"The bat speaks, but the sound waves are too high for . . . humans to hear," the priest said. From a deep pocket Father Francis took out a small white plastic box that looked like a transistor radio.

"This instrument lowers the sound waves." The

priest smiled again. His teeth were cracked and yellow. "Now you will hear the bat speak."

He brought it close to the bat. Suddenly, Marla could hear rapid, whisperlike chattering sounds coming from it while the tiny bat opened and shut its little mouth. "He says it likes you." The bat began to crawl across the palm of the priest's hand. His fingers closed around it, and he put it inside his cassock.

"The land here is ancient. It belongs to . . . people who are different," the priest said quietly. "The native people have lived in the northern forest for thousands of years. Like the bat, they see and hear things that amaze . . . people like you."

"Like wendigos?" Marla challenged the priest, eyeing him steadily.

Father Francis trembled slightly. His head remained bowed, so she still could not see his eyes. She walked closer.

"You've been having dreams," he whispered in a strange sibilant tone so low Marla could barely make out the words. "Dreams of flying. Beautiful dreams. Dreams that make your hunger go away."

Marla was taken aback. She glanced sideways, carefully noting the door to the street ten feet away.

The priest clasped his hands and held them almost prayerlike in front of him. His eyes were still in shadow. "There are places where dreams become conscious, where legends manipulate reality," he said in his soft, whistling voice. His breath had a rank, guttural smell. He raised his head and gazed at her.

"I want to be your friend."

She saw his eyes. A cold sweat broke out across her forehead.

"I have to go," Marla said suddenly. Abruptly, she

made a beeline for the door. She pushed it open, blinking against the bright sunlight outside.

"Don't go! Not yet—"

Marla let the door slam shut on the last of the strange priest's words. She burst into a run, down the street and out of the poor neighborhood, toward Kenora's little shopping district.

Seared in her mind were the priest's eyes, haunted and terrible, filled with an immense and bottomless longing and, just as she had expected, devoid of whites. The pupils were little more than tiny black dots rolling in a sea of blood.

CHAPTER 11

That evening Marla and Kyla had dinner together in the Keewatin's dining room. Small lamps on each table cast warm orange light against the polished log walls, and flames burned lazily in the great stone fireplace. Despite Kyla's urging to eat, Marla picked at her steak.

"Mark Lorrington's taken to wearing his sunglasses while playing tennis," Kyla commented after telling Marla she'd spent almost the entire morning and afternoon on the courts.

"Is he still beating you?"

"Two out of three," Kyla said, faking a tone of indifference. "He's fast. Really fast. I'll be really glad when McKenna shows up Monday and the tennis clinic gets under way. I guess I could use some tips."

Marla looked at Kyla. "I refuse to believe your game is slipping."

Kyla's shoulders rose and fell in time with a big sigh. "It just seems weird that Mark Lorrington is so good and I've never even heard of him before. I mean, he's been around the right clubs, even the right people, so it's not as if he's coming out of nowhere. It's just weird."

They ordered dessert, and Marla played with it, tucking away tiny mouthfuls with her spoon.

"You're quiet tonight," Kyla observed. "How was your trip to downtown Kenora?"

Marla shrugged. "Okay, I guess. Not exactly a shoppers' paradise. I ran into—" She paused, considering how Kyla would react, and decided she didn't care. "A wendigo. I think."

Kyla stopped eating. "Meaning?"

Marla related the encounter with the strange priest at the mission. Even as she spoke she realized that what she omitted from the story was far more significant than the details she mentioned. She didn't tell Kyla about the dreams she was having. And she didn't tell her about the strange sense of familiarity she felt with Father Francis. "It was his eyes," she said, finishing the story. "Massively bloodshot, as though they were rolling in blood."

Kyla looked at her skeptically. "Sounds to me like he saw you on the cover of *Cheeky* and recognized you on the street," she said dismissively, deliberately endorsing Father Francis's explanation. "If he were a wendigo, why didn't he eat you?"

"Maybe he wants to," Marla giggled. "He's just waiting for the right time." She looked down at her uneaten dessert. "You know, I think modeling is a bad idea. I mean, it's like anyone who sees my picture thinks he owns a piece of me."

"Marla, people would kill to do what you're doing."

"I know that," Marla said, suddenly sullen. She set

down her spoon. "I'm just not sure it's what I want to do with my life. I've been doing it since I was a little girl because of my mother. It's like I never really had a choice about it."

"So do something else."

"Sure." Marla pushed her dessert away. "Botany," she said sarcastically. "Or animal husbandry. I'd be a disaster at that. I'd pick the wrong mates every time. Just like I attract the wrong guys."

Kyla looked across the table at Marla and frowned. "What do you mean, you attract them? The problem is that you put up with them instead of telling them to take a walk."

Marla shook her head emphatically. "When I first got here I was totally attracted to Mark Lorrington. Now, well, he kind of scares me, he's such an egotist. Meanwhile Tyrone is the perfect gentleman, but to me that comes off as total wimpiness."

"Even after that vision of northern studliness this morning when he was chopping wood outside his cabin?" Kyla teased.

Marla laughed and shook her head. "You know, that's the first time I saw him in his own environment, and he looked—hot." She stared across the table at Kyla, a bemused smile playing at her lips. "How come we're always talking about my boyfriends and never yours?"

Kyla looked down at her empty dessert plate, her right hand toying with her fork. "Marla, this is really difficult because we've known each other for so long. And I don't know what I'd do if anything happened to our friendship."

Marla looked steadily at her. In a way, she already knew what Kyla was about to tell her. It wasn't a premonition, just a feeling that came from knowing her for so long.

"You know what you said about me not liking guys, well, I do like guys. But not that way. What I mean is, I think I'm gay, Marla. I'm not sure yet, but—" Kyla smiled quickly and bravely. "I like guys a lot, but I really fall for, well, other girls."

Marla swallowed. She fumbled for a response. "Like that famous tennis player—"

"Martina Navratilova? Yeah, I guess so." Kyla tried to read Marla's face. For the first time she could remember, she didn't know what was going on in her friend's head. "You okay?"

"Cool," Marla said almost too briskly. "I get to know lots of gay guys in the modeling business. But I guess I've never met any gay girls before, that's all." She reached across the table and squeezed Kyla's hand. "Kyla, I really admire you for—"

Marla struggled to find the right words. "I was going to say your honesty, you know, for telling me. But really what I admire you for is your honesty with yourself. You've always been as solid as a rock to me."

Kyla blushed. "Me? A rock? You've got to be crazy, Marla. I've always thought you were the strong one. You have more willpower and determination than anyone I know."

"You're kidding!" Marla looked at Kyla with disbelief.

Kyla shook her head. "Sometimes you don't use it the right way, that's all. Like dieting too much."

Marla sighed. "I never thought of it that way." She plucked her napkin from her lap and dropped it on the table. "I feel like I spend so much time trying to be what everyone expects me to be, I'm not even sure who the real Marla is."

Kyla folded her napkin and placed it carefully by her empty plate. "I'm certainly not going to be ashamed of anything, or live my life to please everyone else," she said with quiet determination. "And neither should you."

Just as they were leaving the dining room, something occurred to Marla. For a moment it embarrassed her.

"Kyla, are . . . are you . . ." Marla stammered. "With me . . ."

Kyla gave a little laugh. "All that's important is that you're my oldest and best friend in the world."

Marla hugged her. "Kyla, I just wish I could be as brave as you. About who I am and what I want."

When Kyla opted for a walk along the lake and some fresh air, Marla returned to her room alone. She stepped off the elevator on her floor and turned down the carpeted hallway that led to her room. She had barely inserted her key in the lock and turned it when suddenly Mark Lorrington was standing in front of her, blocking her path.

Disconcerted, Marla stopped. Where had he come from, she wondered—thin air? Despite the time of evening, Mark wore sunglasses, and he had a goofy grin that didn't suit him.

"Are you on drugs or something?" Marla scowled, trying to push past him. He stopped her by slapping his right hand against the wall. When she turned to evade him, he blocked her with his left arm as well, pinning her to the wall. He was leering at her, and she could see her face reflected in his sunglasses, tight and drawn. The skin of Mark's arms, where they brushed her shoulders, was ice cold.

"Y'know, this is exactly what I left New York to get away from," Marla protested angrily.

Mark plunged his lips down on hers, crushing her mouth and pushing the back of her head against the door frame. His hand went to her waist. Marla spun sideways and free from his grasp, suppressing the scream that had risen in her throat. She wiped her mouth with the back of her hand. He was freezing cold. It was like kissing the dead. And he was staring at her with that stupid smile on his face, as if he expected a reward or something. She bit her lip and pushed past him, into her room. She slammed the door shut and bolted it firmly.

In the corridor Mark's features contorted into anger. "Tease," he muttered. He couldn't resist reaching out to grip the doorknob, squeezing his fist around it, turning it slowly until it clicked. He shoved his weight against the door, turned the doorknob back and forth rapidly, imagining Marla's terror. Then he let go and swaggered self-consciously away, as if baleful eyes, watching through peepholes in the walls and ceiling, had witnessed his triumph as a man.

In her room Marla stared in terror as the door handle rotated back and forth. When he shoved against the wooden panels, she barely suppressed a scream. Then she heard his footsteps retreat down the corridor. She threw her bag onto the bed, stripped off her jacket, and went into the bathroom with its glistening white porcelain fixtures and polished chrome fittings. She opened the window, and an icy wind swept in, rattling the glasses on the shelf above the sink, flapping the plastic curtains around the large enamel tub.

Her stomach felt as if it were clamped between steel claws. She turned on the cold water tap. Without waiting to fill a glass, she bent down and drank from it, guzzling the cold water back until her teeth were freezing. Her heart was pounding.

After she had thrown up, she fell back, weak and disoriented, sprawled upon the tile floor in a cold sweat. From the corner of her eye she saw a whirlwind of glittering snow spinning in the open window like a small vortex. She told herself it wasn't the season for snow, but still it hovered there, spinning back and forth along the sill. She heard a voice whispering in a singsong tone:

She is beautiful, she is pretty.
She is the queen of the golden city.

And she knew the wendigo was calling her, the voice she recognized from her sweet dreams at night, dreams of flying over the dark northern landscape. The voice of Father Francis.

And just as it did in her dreams, it comforted her, offering her a new life, an existence different from the one she hated. Then she felt ice, a wonderful white-sugar coldness, like a dentist's anesthetic, seeping into her veins, into her bones, numbing her, freezing her unhappiness, abolishing the misery she felt from hating what her life had become.

She went to bed with the windows wide open and the curtains swirling in the icy breezes, content to know that she would dream again.

Mark made his way through the Keewatin's maze of service corridors to the back door off the kitchens. He knew that he was changing because of the dreams he was having. Nothing that anyone would notice yet. Fine downy hair covered his body, and two lumps pressed against the skin on either side of his forehead just under the hairline. When he cut himself, he no longer bled. And the wound healed in a matter of hours. As for his powers, he was just beginning to know what they were. He could move faster and faster, a skill that on the tennis courts had allowed him to beat Kyla Recki in almost every game. And he had started to hear people's thoughts, like a whispering white noise constant in the background.

There were greater powers to enjoy. Wendigos were shape-shifters and they could fly. They controlled people by infiltrating their thoughts. All these were talents Mark could make use of. The only thing that scared him just a little was a nagging question: Was it worth the price? Indeed, what exactly was the price other than a sensitivity to bright light and this feeling in his gut, hunger cramps that food did not satisfy?

He emerged into a cool spring night, redolent with the smell of pine, and luminescent with moonlight. He took the path that led toward Tyrone's cabin. Tyrone had always been a little too serious about the wendigo. It was time to give his friend a demonstration.

Tall blue pines lined the path, their branches wavering in the light breeze. Mark heard a whisper behind his right ear. He turned sharply, adrenaline instantly flooding his system. No one was there. There was only darkness under the heavy, swaying branches of the pines. The pounding of his heart began to ebb, and he walked on.

A few steps later he heard the whispering in his left ear, as if someone had rotated the balance switch on a stereo. Nothing was there. Suddenly Mark was seized by a bone-chilling certainty. Before, it came in dreams. This was real.

He began to run. Too late.

The wendigo swooped down, one great bulbous foot with its single toe touching the ground and instantly rebounding with Mark clenched tightly in its massive, hairy arms.

Frozen by abject terror, pinned in the nightmare embrace of a monster twice his size, Mark saw the sprawling roofs of the Keewatin zooming away far below, the hotel's grounds, the lake, the lights of Kenora, and then the great northern forest sprawling in darkness to the horizon, the tiny waters of thousands of lakes like leaden splotches.

The smell of rot and decay struck his nostrils and burned his throat and nose. His eyes stung and he gasped for air, but the wendigo flew higher, until the lights of cities were visible, clusters of twinkling diamonds scattered across the inky blackness of North America. Higher still, the whole continent was beneath him, the eastern seaboard perfectly outlined against the dark Atlantic by the lights along the coast. And then the orb of earth spun below, and satellites whizzed past, flickering reflections of light spinning off their burnished metal pods.

His arms and legs burned with agonizing pain, as if they had been set on fire, but Mark could not scream because he could no longer breathe. There was no oxygen. His chest was paralyzed. He squirmed and began to asphyxiate. The monster's face bent toward Mark's, its yellow teeth broken like ancient rock, its ragged lips torn into flaps of horrible flesh. Unable to scream, unable to do anything, Mark felt the wendigo's mouth come down on his and expel a great, decaying breath.

Instantly, his air-starved body relaxed. A numbing coldness seeped from his lungs into his veins, cooling the blood and vanishing into the bone, where his marrow froze instantly. Saliva flooded into his mouth. Mark felt hungry. Ravenous. He wanted to eat, to grow enormous.

As if sensing Mark's need, the wendigo shifted course and plunged back into the atmosphere. Mark saw the continents of Asia circling below, the great expanse of the Pacific, the coast of North America, mountains, then the line where prairie wheat fields met the great rocky expanse of the Canadian Shield. He was flying at enormous speed just above the tips of fir and spruce, in a landscape of trees that swept to the horizon. A lake dotted with islands opened up below him. Ahead on the farther shore were lights that he recognized as the town of Kenora.

Mark felt himself tossed aside like a rag doll. He thudded limply against soft wet ground but felt no pain. He was aware that it was still night, and smelled the forest. Ice-cold water from the wet ground was seeping through his clothing. He liked the feeling. But he was hungry.

He pushed himself up on his hands and knees. His mouth opened and shut involuntary, and he gnashed his teeth and grunted. The air was filled with the stench of putrefying meat. Not far away he saw the spread-eagled body of a man, belly up, except there was no belly. The body had been ripped open. Intestines were strewn across the clearing like sausage.

The wendigo stood over it, a towering silhouette outlined by stars, covered with hair, long, thin antlers sprouting from its gnarled forehead. The monster moved quickly, tearing the limbs from the torso. In a flash it moved forward and dropped something in front of Mark.

It was a man's arm, crushed and broken. Spit dripped from Mark's mouth. It was what he needed, and desperately. He grabbed it, drew the human flesh to his lips. Blood poured into him, and began to fill him, fresh, delicious, and scalding hot.

CHAPTER 12

Just after dawn Tyrone left his cabin on the grounds of the Keewatin, his fishing gear in hand, and set out toward the lake. He didn't have to report for work at the hotel until eight, which left him almost two hours of quiet time. He cut through a swath of pine trees and saw Mark, standing in the path, his jacket covered with mud. He was circling as if lost.

Tyrone dropped his fishing gear and ran to his friend's side. Mark staggered and fell against him. Tyrone hooked his arms under Mark's shoulders to support him.

"Must have been some party," Tyrone muttered disapprovingly. There had been occasions like this in Los Angeles, when Mark disappeared for a night of hard partying, and Tyrone had to cover for him. But feeling Mark's weight sag against him, Tyrone realized his friend was as cold as ice. He noticed Mark's T-shirt, drenched by a great red stain.

"Man, you've got blood all over you!"

Mark looked up at him, his eyes dazed and bloodshot. "I'm gonna *rule,* dude! Gonna—" His head sagged, and he repeated his words, slurring them and letting them trail off.

"C'mon, I'll get you to bed so you can sleep this off." Supporting Mark, Tyrone made his way across the lawn to a side door of the Keewatin, and a service elevator. When they reached the Lorrington family suite, Tyrone dumped him on his bed and started undressing him.

Mark's eyes fluttered open. "So high, sooo beautifullll," he babbled deliriously.

Tyrone stripped off Mark's jeans and the bloody T-shirt. His friend's skin was blue from wandering in the cold, and his toes and fingers were white from frostbite. He checked Mark carefully for wounds. There were none. The blood was not his. *An animal,* Tyrone wondered. He asked softly, "Mark, what the hell were you doing all night?"

Mark's eyes opened, and he stared at Tyrone. His face twisted as if he were wincing from a great pain. His answer was a long-drawn-out moan. "Can't breathe! These fiery heights, my feet of fire, my burning feet of fire!"

Marla was awakened by a knock on her door but resisted getting out of bed to answer it. She had flown in her dreams again, vividly, across the northern landscape, over forests and lakes, oceans and continents. She had felt content, and even more, in the strange logic that dreams have, she had been safe, from what or by what means, she had no idea.

The knocks on the door sounded again, this time more insistent. She threw back the covers and sat up.

The window was wide open. Her alarm clock indicated it was after ten.

"Just a second," she called out. She grabbed her bathrobe and went to the door. It was Kyla, her eyes afire and, uncharacteristically, pouting.

"He's not coming!" she announced angrily, moving into the room. "He's canceled out."

Marla looked at her a second before it sank in. "Oh. You mean Tom McKenna?"

"Yes, I mean him," Kyla shot back. "And all because he lost his temper and threw his racquet around. This whole thing has been a total waste of time!"

"Not total," Marla said. "I've been having wonderful dreams since we came here." She went to the windows and started to close them, noticing how bright the sun was. New York was so far away. She wanted to stay at the Keewatin a few more days. It was for a reason, she knew, and yet it was almost inexplicable. It was something she had to finish, although for the life of her, she didn't know what it was. "Let's go for breakfast and figure out what we're going to do next."

Breakfast service was available on the Keewatin's terrace, just outside the French doors that led from the dining room. On a Sunday morning in the off season, it seemed like they were the only guests.

"So have any of the other kids in the tennis clinic shown up?" Marla asked.

Kyla shook her head sullenly. "Nope. They all had time to cancel when they got the news. Two got as far as Winnipeg and turned back. There's just us here now. It feels creepy."

A waiter brought them juice and coffee. Marla gazed out over the Keewatin's spacious lawns and the sapphire-blue lake, squinting against the sunlight. She reached into her handbag for her sunglasses.

"Have you been crying?" Kyla asked, a question that popped out of the blue.

Marla looked surprised. "No. Why?"

"Your eyes are bloodshot."

She put on her sunglasses and shrugged. "Allergies, maybe. Oh, look who's coming," she said disdainfully, glancing past Kyla.

Kyla glimpsed over her shoulder and saw Mark Lorrington walk onto the terrace. He wore sunglasses and his skin was pale, but a grin spread across his face when he saw the girls. He strode across the terrace to their table.

"Can I join you for a second?" he asked, looking from Marla to Kyla.

Marla stared at him coldly for a second, then turned away. "Don't," she said pointedly.

Mark shuffled uncomfortably and spoke to Kyla. "Guess you heard McKenna's canceled out?"

"I heard," Kyla said tersely. She looked curiously at Marla, wondering about her hostile reaction.

Mark turned to Marla. "I'm really, really sorry for being such a jerk last night." He looked at Kyla and said by way of explanation. "I made a pass at Marla. Sort of."

"You're right about sort of," Marla said tightly.

"Look, I was really dumb. I got into the liquor cabinet in my father's suite, and well . . . you were sort of right, I wasn't on drugs, but I'd been drinking."

"I didn't know you were old enough to drink," Marla shot back.

"I'm not." Mark looked genuinely ashamed. "Like I

said, I was really dumb. And I'm really sorry for how I behaved. You deserve a lot more respect than that."

Marla was more than a little astonished at Mark's transformation. "Your apology is accepted," she said finally.

"So what are your plans now that the tennis clinic is history."

"History that never happened," Kyla commented wryly. "We were just about to talk about that. I suppose we should get back to school in New York."

"On the other hand, we arranged to have the next week off," Marla pointed out. "It's not as if they're expecting us."

"Now that you're here, why don't you hang out," Mark suggested. "Look, I know a beautiful place to camp in Lake of the Woods, but you can get there only by boat. So let's go on an overnight canoe trip. The four of us, including Tyrone." He added, casting a quick glance at Marla, "With separate tents."

Mark took off his sunglasses and looked from Marla to Kyla. His eyes were bloodshot. Kyla looked at Marla to discern what her friend wanted. Marla had reservations, but when she tried to speak she seemed unable to say the words. Mark stared at her intently. Like a robot, Marla heard herself say, "Okay. Why not?"

Kyla was surprised when Marla accepted Mark's offer. "Sure," she said, shrugging carelessly. "I'm up for it if Marla is."

Tyrone was on his way through the Keewatin's vast lobby, delivering a bundle of newspapers to his mother's shop, when he did a double take. Mark Lorrington and Marla were walking in from the terrace. Only five hours earlier Mark had been raving, and even in L.A. it normally took him a day to sleep off his all-night extravaganzas.

Kyla came out of the Gracious Loon and saw the disturbed look on Tyrone's face. "What's up?"

Tyrone swung the bundle of newspapers down next to the stand outside the entrance. "Five hours ago Mark was plastered. I thought he'd be sleeping it off."

"Yeah, he said he got drunk last night."

"Is that what he said?" Tyrone said sharply. He reached into his pocket for a knife and slit the cord binding the newspapers.

"So you guys going back to New York now that McKenna's not coming?"

Kyla shook her head. "Not till after the canoe trip."

"What canoe trip?" Tyrone looked at her, surprised.

"Mark asked us. We're leaving this afternoon."

"*Mark* asked you!" Tyrone exclaimed. "And you agreed!"

Kyla was taken aback by Tyrone's overreaction. "Marla wanted to. And we don't have to be back at school until next week." She looked at him. "You're supposed to be going too. I guess Mark hasn't told you yet."

"I'm supposed to work," he said tightly, ripping the wrapping off the bundle of newspapers. The headline was big and bold, and screamed back at them: *Mutilated Body Found.*

"Oh, God," Kyla breathed, watching Tyrone pick up the paper and glance at the article. She saw a picture taken in the forest, a pool of blood in the grass, policemen searching for clues. "Don't tell Marla. She'll freak."

Tyrone folded up the paper and thought of the blood on Mark's T-shirt. No, he told himself. It was impossible. He gazed across the cavernous timbered hall of the

Keewatin. Mark and Marla stood near the doors to the terrace, still in animated conversation. A shaft of light framed their silhouettes. Marla's hair looked like a halo of gold. A breeze circulated, tossing the sheer curtains.

He folded the blade of his pocket knife and slipped it back in his jeans pocket. Mark was up to something. "I'll get the time off," Tyrone told Kyla. "I wouldn't miss this canoe trip for the world."

CHAPTER 13

Mark decided to have the camping trip catered by the Keewatin's kitchen. There was enough food to feed an army, as well as two tents, a naphtha stove, water bottles, lanterns, life jackets, and two green cedar-strip canoes strapped to the roof rack of the Jeep. They were in the service parking lot behind the hotel, and just about ready to leave.

"That about does it," Mark said, testing the knots on the ropes holding the canoes.

Marla slid into the backseat and felt something hard and flat underneath her. She reached down and pulled out an enormous machete in a leather sheath.

"I thought these were for jungles," she called to Mark, waving it out the window.

Mark grabbed it from her, and then gave her a forced smile to temper his sudden reaction. "You'd be amazed how useful that is—anywhere." He went around to the back of the Jeep and packed it away.

Tyrone appeared, striding up the path from his cabin, a knapsack slung over his shoulder. He carried his long-handled ax in one hand.

Kyla joined Marla in the backseat. "Boys and their toys," she sighed, observing Tyrone's ax through the windshield.

"I brought a hatchet, so we don't really need that," Mark announced when Tyrone pulled up beside him. He pointed at the ax. "I mean, we're only building a couple of campfires."

Tyrone hefted it, his hand just under the sharp steel head. "You never know when a real ax will come in handy though." He crammed it into the back of the Jeep with everything else.

With Mark at the wheel and Tyrone navigating, they drove north and soon hit gravel roads. For a while the scenery was monotonous, the road slashing straight through a forest of tangled spruce, with the Jeep leaving a heavy plume of gravel dust in its trail. Even with the windows closed a thin layer of fine dust soon covered everything in the interior. Occasionally, they passed lakes, glimpses of cool blue water where the trees thinned, or the tall yellow cattails of marshes. But except for the road and the long line of electricity poles that ran in single file along one side, there was no sign of human habitation.

The road entered a stretch of blackened stumps, the charred remains of a forest fire that had swept through several years earlier. Dead trees poked at odd angles from a carpet of green, new life that had already grown up in the ashes of the old. The fire had burned for miles, wreaking its destruction to the edge of the horizon. Here and there in the distance were patches of green, bits of forest that had survived the fire through the whim of wind.

With the sun baking in the closed windows, the air was hot and stultifying. Marla opened hers a crack and enjoyed the cool, fresh breeze.

"There's a settlement store up ahead, and we need to buy naphtha for the lanterns," Tyrone announced, turning around from the passenger seat in front. "Then we turn off."

They came to an intersection, where a narrow road came out of the forest and crossed the one they were on. On one side the land began to rise to rolling, forested hills, the first of which loomed over them, not far in the distance. Telephone poles at each corner were covered with rows of hand-painted signs pointing to lakes and cabins in every direction. One indicated an Ojibway reservation several miles up the road. On another corner the forest had been bulldozed away, leaving scarred gravel hills around a ramshackle frame store with gas pumps out front. The parking area was empty when they drove into the lot. A shaggy old dog ran out from under the porch, barking furiously.

Mark and Tyrone were models of efficiency. Mark started filling the gas tank and Tyrone headed for the store for the naphtha. "Check this place out," he told Marla and Kyla. "It's like going back to another century or something."

They went up the steps onto the covered porch, where cases containing hundreds of dusty soft-drink bottles were stacked everywhere. A row of deer heads and antlers had been mounted on the outside wall. The wooden façade on both sides of the front door was stapled with notices for fishing licenses, land for sale, and a post office. Tyrone waved the girls ahead.

The rickety door shook and a bell jangled when Marla pushed it open. The store was one giant room with shelves built along the walls and up to the ceilings, holding everything from clothing to canned goods, galvanized iron washtubs and kerosene lanterns, fishing lures, leather gloves and rubber boots, coils of ropes, and tools of all descriptions. The floor was cut by two long aisles, and tables stacked with even more merchandise lined them. The profusion was overwhelming.

Tyrone headed toward a counter at the back of the store, where a white man and a native woman sat in old wooden chairs. Marla started wandering through the rows of merchandise. Kyla waited near the door, scanning a bulletin-board that advertised cottages and camps for sale. On one side was a wanted poster with mug shots of the broad face of a native man, full-face and in profile. His neck was thick but his high cheekbones gave him a regal appearance. He had long black hair falling back over his shoulders, and his eyes drilled out of the poster at her. Underneath the pictures was the name: Willie Beaver, wanted for murder.

Through the glass window in the door Kyla saw a car drive into the lot, an old Buick from the late sixties, long, heavy, and riding low on broken shocks. The fenders had rusted, and the paint was burned away from years of sun and snow. It stopped on the other side of the gas pumps from the Jeep.

Mark came in the door and saw Kyla. "Willie Beaver," he said almost gleefully. "That's the wendigo who ate his family."

Tyrone, walking down a nearby aisle, overheard. "Drop it, Mark," he said sharply.

"Drop what?" Mark challenged him.

Tyrone looked quickly around the store and saw Marla buying something at the counter and out of hearing distance.

"All this wendigo stuff," he said quietly. "It upsets Marla."

Mark gazed at him, unaffected, his chin jutting out belligerently. "So you're Marla's protector now?"

Footsteps on the porch outside diverted their attention. Six native men had piled out of the car, and three of them were on their way into the store.

"Just drop it, Mark," Tyrone repeated in a low, even voice.

At the other end of the store, the man called for Tyrone and held up a can of naphtha. The door jangled opened and the native men pushed inside. They glared when they saw the three teenagers, but ignored them.

"I'll wait outside," Kyla announced to Mark and Tyrone, grabbing the door before it closed. She stepped onto the porch and went down the steps to wait for the others by the Jeep.

Three native men stood beside the car. Two were talking. The third looked at Kyla. Jet-black hair fell straight down his back, and his broad face with its high, prominent cheekbones seemed prematurely aged.

It was Willie Beaver.

Their eyes met, and Kyla froze. His face remained impassive. His eyes stared directly into hers, dark and piercing, with fierce red rims.

Rolling in blood, Kyla thought, remembering Tyrone's description of wendigos. She was aware of how odd the moment seemed, as if the air had suddenly become suffocating. She couldn't move. She struggled against the immobility of her limbs, but felt completely paralyzed. For a moment the glimmer of a smile teased at Willie Beaver's lips. His eyes looked gentle, almost kindly.

He turned away. Kyla's heart beat furiously and blood pounded into her head. The other two natives took the fugitive by the elbow and turned him toward the car, one blocking him, the other opening the rear door. To Kyla, everyone moved in slow motion, as if she were watching a dream unfold.

The native men inside the store came out, carrying bags of groceries and a drum marked KEROSENE. They tramped down the steps and strode across the gravel toward the big old car. Kyla looked at the door, waiting for Marla, Tyrone, or Mark to come out. The Buick's doors slammed heavily, and the motor started. Kyla saw Willie Beaver through the rear window, sitting in the backseat, sandwiched between two men. He turned, his eyes caught hers, this time with an expression of monumental sadness.

The Buick's rear wheels spun for a moment in gravel, then caught. The car bucked out of the lot and onto the road. She watched it turn in the direction of the Ojibway reservation, quickly swallowed by a dragon of gravel dust.

A clatter of footsteps on the plank floor of the veranda made her jump. She turned, suddenly able to move again. Marla, Tyrone, and Mark tripped down the steps. Tyrone carried a metal can of liquid naphtha.

"What's the matter?" Mark said, walking around to the driver's door.

She was about to tell them what she'd seen, but something stopped her. She felt as if the words disappeared from her throat before they could be spoken.

"Nothing," Kyla answered finally. A moment ago she was sure it was Willie Beaver. Now she wasn't. She told herself she was imagining things. "Nothing at all," she repeated uncertainly before climbing back into the Jeep.

CHAPTER 14

They drove for almost another hour, moving slowly on a bumpy road. It wound up and down over hills, around sheer rock faces, and dipped into somber swamps that spread through acres of low-lying forest. The stumps and limbs of drowned trees, stripped of bark, emerged from shallow, murky water like a landscape of bones. Then they began to climb again, driving over rock and past craggy fir trees perched on hillsides.

The road ended abruptly at a sandy beach, and a view of Lake of the Woods that stretched to the horizon. The waters were cool blue, and the lake was dotted with hundreds of islands, some barely more than a rock poking above the water with a few tall grasses and a single tree. Mark and Tyrone hauled the canoes from the roof rack and carried them to the water's edge.

"How do you row with these things?" Marla asked, hoisting a varnished paddle and examining it curiously.

"You don't row canoes, you paddle them," Tyrone laughed. "Like this." He took the paddle from her, wrapped his hand over the knob at the top, and put his other hand halfway down the shaft. "You'll get the hang of it. Probably a few blisters too."

Kyla and Mark took one canoe, while Marla and Tyrone set out in the other. Marla sat in the bow, paddling delicately. In the stern Tyrone dipped his paddle and pushed the water back with a J stroke to steer the canoe out into the lake.

They hugged the shoreline, with Tyrone and Marla leading. They looked back toward shore, where the forests, rising up the sides of the rocky hills, had a solemn majesty. The late afternoon sun threw out a final burst of yellow heat, and they dallied near a swamp, where a beaver's dam was visible between the trunks of dead trees. The water broke in front of the canoe, and Marla saw a flash of iridescent blue.

"A beaver!" Tyrone laughed with delight. "All you saw was the tail."

Farther down the lake, the shoreline changed dramatically from low-lying forest to rocky cliffs that loomed over the water, forty feet high. Long, cool afternoon shadows turned the waters of the lake a deep jade-green. They paddled in close, and Tyrone pointed to the cracks and fissures that covered the vertical surface of the rock.

"The native people still put little packages of tobacco into these cracks," he explained. "It's some kind of offering to the spirits of the mountain."

They paddled away from the cliffs, Tyrone leading

them toward a heavily forested peninsula that jutted into the lake. As they approached they saw a tent, and a canoe pulled up on the shore. Two young native men squatted over a fire. On the rocks nearby, fishing lines had been set in the water, the poles anchored into little mounds of rock. Tyrone waved, and led the canoes around the peninsula to the other side, where the flat shore stretched out into the water.

Tyrone and Mark hauled the canoes onto shore and quickly set up camp, staking the pup tents and gathering wood. Tyrone chopped kindling and built a campfire. The sun was lowering steadily in the west, casting a rose-red glow across the lake, and turning the forest into darkness.

Mark returned from a foray to the woods with several sturdy sticks that ended in forked branches. Swinging his machete in quick, even blows, he quickly peeled the bark, cut them to size, and stuck them in the ground on each side of the campfire.

Tyrone lit the kindling and coaxed the fire into a roaring blaze. They watched the sunset and felt the coolness come down with the end of day. When the fire had burned to coals, Tyrone impaled a chicken with a long stick and set it on the forked stakes. While the smells of roasting chicken wafted over the campsite, Marla and Kyla unpacked the rest of the food and set out a feast. For once Marla let herself eat voraciously, her appetite fueled by the fresh air, and the long, active day.

After eating they cleared away the food, packing it away in a plastic cooler. Marla dug a bulky sweater out of her knapsack and slipped it on over her jacket. It was cool, and the scent of wood smoke mingled with the smells of the pines. Overhead, in the black night sky, trillions of stars glittered, reflecting on the lake and suffusing the air with a ghostly luminescence.

Marla approached the campfire, where Kyla and Tyrone sat to keep warm. Mark was puttering with something at the edge of the woods, and showed no inclination to join them. They stared into the flames, a hypnotic silence falling among them. Mark approached from the shadows at the edge of the forest but still hung back from the fire. The coolness didn't seem to bother him. He was wearing only his T-shirt.

"You're not going to believe this," Kyla said after a long period of silence. "But today at that little store I thought I saw that killer in the car that pulled in while we were there." It had been tormenting Kyla ever since, tearing her between disbelief and a duty to inform the police.

"What killer?" Marla asked.

"Willie Beaver. I saw his photograph on a wanted poster on the bulletin-board inside. And when I walked outside, he was standing with the native men from that old car."

Tyrone looked at her curiously. "You're right. I don't believe you."

Mark stepped closer to the fire. "Beaver? He's a wendigo."

Tyrone looked at him with annoyance.

"He was standing outside by the car when I went out," Kyla insisted.

"You imagined it," Marla suggested.

"Come on now, Kyla," Mark taunted. "All those Indians look the same to us, don't they."

"That's racist, Mark," Kyla hissed angrily.

Mark walked closer. The firelight flickered orange across his face. He started reciting:

The Wendigo!
The Wendigo!
I saw it just a friend ago!
Last night it lurked in Canada;
Tonight, on your veranada!

"Stop it!" Tyrone ordered, looking quickly at Marla and unable to conceal his annoyance any longer.

"Stop what, Tyrone?" Mark demanded, his voice taunting. "Stop saying *wendigo* out loud? What's the matter, Tyrone, are you superstitious? You think the wendigo might actually come?" He snickered scornfully. "You think I'm a wendigo?"

Tyrone looked boldly at Mark. His eyes were dark. "I'm starting to wonder."

"Maybe it's not such a bad thing, being a wendigo," Mark shot back. "Being able to run so fast you can fly. Using mind control to make people do what you want them to."

"Wendigos are cannibals," Tyrone said darkly. "They kill people and eat them. You want to be a cannibal, Mark?"

"I want to be a predator, Tyrone. Not like most people who go out to supermarkets and buy their dead meat all wrapped up in plastic after someone else has done their killing for them. Like scavengers. Vultures and jackals." Mark looked around the campfire at his three friends. He jabbed his thumb at his chest. "A predator hunts and kills his own food. The strong devour the weak. Like lions. And grizzlies." Mark turned and stared at Tyrone. "And wendigos."

Kyla giggled nervously. "Personally, I've been considering vegetarianism."

Mark laughed, and the sound of it echoed across the

lake. It was a strange laugh, cruel and mocking. "Enjoy the campfire," he told them. "I'm going out in the canoe."

Without a backward glance he stalked toward the shore, where the canoes rested just above the water's edge.

Tyrone stood up, brushing dirt and twigs from the seat of his pants. "I'll be right back," he told Marla and Kyla. He followed Mark down to the lake.

Mark was carrying one of the canoes to the water. He set it down, anchoring it with one end on the rocky shore. He ignored Tyrone's greeting. Tyrone reached out and put his hand on his friend's shoulder. Mark turned sharply and pushed it away. He glared at Tyrone with a look that bordered on hatred.

"Mark, you've got to tell me what's going on," Tyrone said softly, almost pleading. "When I found you this morning you had blood on your shirt. Man, you've got to tell me!"

"Nothing to tell," Mark sneered.

"If you're in trouble, I want to help you."

Mark threw his head back and laughed. "Help me? I don't need any help from you, Tyrone. I just had the biggest break in my life handed to me. You'll see. You and those babes." He gestured with his chin toward Marla and Kyla, thirty feet away.

An uncomfortable silence fell between the two young men. Mark waited defiantly, his bloodshot eyes narrowed and a strange, secretive smirk creasing his face. Finally, Tyrone spoke slowly and deliberately.

"If you try anything—anything dangerous—so help me, Mark, I'll kill you if I have to."

Mark snickered. "Listen to the big, studly man. If you try, Tyrone. I'll tear you to pieces." He opened his eyes wider and stared intensely at Tyrone. Tyrone blinked and tried to turn away. He couldn't. He was frozen, unable to move, even to talk.

Mark stared with wide, bloodshot eyes. Then he laughed and broke the spell. He pushed the canoe farther into the water and hopped in just as it cleared the shore.

Tyrone realized he could move again. He stepped quickly to the water's edge. "Mark!"

Mark ignored him. With several swift dips of Mark's paddle, the canoe gained speed and became little more than a dark shadow over the water. Then it disappeared altogether. Tyrone watched for a moment, doubt and fear gnawing at his gut. He shivered, and was suddenly aware that he had broken out in a cold sweat. Mark had done that to him—paralyzed him. He knew it wasn't his imagination. Slowly, Tyrone walked back to the campfire.

"I don't know what's gotten into him," Tyrone said almost apologetically when he approached Marla and Kyla.

"It's no big deal, Tyrone," Kyla said.

Marla listened to the wind seep through the pine trees, swaying the branches overhead. She wondered if she would dream again that she was flying. "I'm beat," she announced. "I'm turning in."

Tyrone waited by the fire, watching for Mark's return while Marla and Kyla retreated to their sleeping bags in one of the pup tents. Silence gripped the clearing, and the fire died down until it was barely a mound of coals and white ash. Tyrone reached for his ax and slipped a sharpening stone from the pocket of his plaid jacket. Quietly and carefully, he drew it along the edge of the gleaming blade. He passed his thumb gently over the edge to test it. Eventually he was satisfied. Mark still wasn't back. Tyrone crawled into the other tent, taking the ax with him. He zipped up his sleeping bag and tucked the ax beneath him, his hand gripped firmly around the shaft.

Kyla's eyes snapped open. She had been asleep, but she didn't know for how long. A dense, rotten smell penetrated the little tent. Beside her, Marla was curled up in her sleeping bag, her chest rising and falling evenly with her breathing. Kyla heard movement outside. She peered through a slit in the nylon door.

The last quarter moon had risen low on the horizon, and in the clear silvery light she saw Mark walk across the clearing. His machete was imbedded in a log not far from the remains of the fire. He gripped the handle and pulled it out. Then he started into the forest beyond the campsite.

Kyla pulled on her running shoes and slipped out of the tent, calling softly to him. He disappeared among the trees. Kyla ran after him. At the edge of the forest she listened to him moving, branches crashing and twigs cracking underfoot. She called again. The noise stopped. She heard him whisper.

"Over here, Kyla."

"Mark?" Kyla stepped into the forest. "Mark, are you all right?" Dregs of moonlight filtered down through the tree branches, barely illuminating the forest floor.

She heard him move, this time off to her right. She walked a few steps in that direction, and called again.

"This way, Kyla!" Mark's voice beckoned her and once again she heard the noise of his passage. "I'm over here," he called again, farther in the forest. Again she followed the sound of branches breaking underfoot.

Kyla could not remember when she lost track of her path into the forest. Mark stopped calling to her, and she could no longer hear him move. She decided to retrace her steps back to the campsite. She walked and walked, her anxiety growing. She realized she should have reached the campsite by then. She turned and tried walking in another direction, stumbling over fallen logs. Branches whipped at her face and arms. She stopped to take stock of her surroundings, the black silhouettes of trees and the impenetrable shadows beyond. She had no idea which way the lake or the camp was. She was hopelessly lost.

Curled up in his sleeping bag, Tyrone dreamed that he was flying. He felt his body pulled upward by some inexorable force, sucked from the ground and winged across cold, dark skies. He was deathly cold. He fought the clutches of the strange, alien evil that controlled him, and heard a scream, thin as wire: *Oh, my feet of fire, my burning feet of fire.*

Panic shook him, terror rising in his chest. He tried to make himself fall back to earth, but whatever gripped him refused to let go. He told himself he was dreaming.

Suddenly, he felt as if he were swimming upward from deep water, barely able to breathe. He was holding something. He brought his hand up and saw the ax. Someone screamed.

He opened his eyes and gasped for air. Marla's face hovered over his.

"Tyrone! It's me!" Her eyes were frozen in horror, and she had her hands up to fend off the blow.

Tyrone froze, the blade of the ax poised inches from Marla's head. He choked back a cry and pulled away from her. "Oh, God, I'm sorry, Marla," he said, catching his breath and blinking to clear his eyes of sleep. "I was dreaming, I—"

"Kyla's gone and Mark hasn't come back yet!" Marla interrupted. She was kneeling beside him in the low tent. The first white light of dawn glowed through the mosquito-net windows.

Tyrone kicked back his sleeping bag. He was instantly alert.

"You almost killed me," Marla said, glancing at the ax.

"Did you see Kyla go?" Tyrone demanded.

Marla shook her head. "I woke up just a few minutes ago. Her sleeping bag's cold. She's been gone for a while."

Tyrone grabbed his sneakers and quickly laced them up. He and Marla crawled out of the tent, and saw Mark. He was standing at the edge of the camp, splattered with blood from head to toe. He walked forward, stiff-legged, his eyes like headlights. In one hand he held what looked like a human limb. In the other he gripped his machete, slicing it back and forth through the air.

"I got hungry, and those Indians looked good to eat," Mark growled. His voice reverberated across the campsite, unnaturally loud. He dropped the limb. It was a man's arm, hacked from the body at the shoulder. He stepped closer. The machete whistled back and forth through the chill dawn air.

Tyrone raised the ax and clenched it tightly with both hands. "Mark, throw down the machete," he warned. "I don't want to hurt you. We can get you help, you have to believe that!"

Mark laughed, but it sounded forced. "I don't need help, Tyrone. I need to eat!"

Mark lunged at Tyrone like a wild animal, bringing the machete down at his head.

"Stop it!" Marla shrieked.

Tyrone hurled himself sideways, bringing the ax up to ward off the blow. The machete blade struck the metal head with the ring of steel against steel. The blow vibrated through the ax handle, stinging Tyrone's hand. He moved quickly, using the blunt back side of the blade and pounding it into Mark's gut.

Instead of reeling over in pain, Mark absorbed the blow and grinned wildly at Tyrone. He stepped forward, the machete swinging like a scythe. Tyrone backed up and tripped over a fallen log.

Instantly Mark was over him, the machete raised high above his head. Marla screamed. Tyrone brought the ax handle in front of him barely in time. The machete's cruel blade bit into the wooden shaft, almost severing it in two. Tyrone rolled sideways and leapt to his feet. He swung the ax.

The blade hit Mark's shoulder and sank several inches into his flesh. The machete fell from his hand. He jumped back, grabbing his weapon up from the ground with the other hand. His eyes had a feral glow. He spat. Tyrone looked at the neat wound across Mark's shoulder. Something was wrong. There was no blood.

Mark screamed horribly, raising the machete over his head and coming at Tyrone. Tyrone swung. The ax bit into Mark's other arm, knocking him sideways. He stumbled against a tent and let out a shrill, ear-piercing shriek. For a second he glared at Tyrone, growling like a cornered animal. Then he turned and ran frantically into the forest, still clenching the machete.

Tyrone was aware that he was panting hard. Marla sobbed uncontrollably nearby. He caught his breath and brought his ax up to look at the steel head. There was no blood from Mark's horrible wounds. Instead, the sharp steel blade glistened with fine red crystals of ice.

CHAPTER 15

A cold silence fell from the forest. Marla stared at the menacing line of trees, where the shadows hid terror. Behind them was the lake, and escape.

"We have to find Kyla!"

"No, Marla!" Tyrone grabbed her as she started for the forest. Marla struggled to break free, but he held her firmly around the waist and shook her. "He's stronger than us, and he'll attack. You have to trust me!"

Marla sagged. "What, then?"

"We have to get help!" Tyrone pushed her toward the canoes at the edge of the lake. "Get in," he ordered, watching the forest carefully as he held the canoe steady. He handed her one of the paddles. When she was sitting in the bow he pushed the canoe out and leapt across several feet of water into the stern. He dug his paddle deep into the water, and the canoe gathered speed, coasting out on the silent lake.

"Paddle!" he yelled.

Numbly, Marla lifted her paddle and dipped it in the water.

"Again! Harder!"

Marla gritted her teeth and dug the blade deep into the water, pulling it back with all her strength. She did it again and again, until the hysteria that had been squeezing her heart like a hand began to ease with the steady rhythm. Tyrone seemed to know this. Over and over she heard his voice calling to her from the stern, telling her that everything would be all right.

By the time they were out in the lake, the rising sun had turned the sky crimson and reflected across the rippling water like molten flesh. Tyrone knew exactly where to go. There was an RCMP detachment at a settlement two miles up the lake. It soon came into view, several boat houses and a score of cabins arrayed along the shore, with the ever-present forest pressing up behind. A small airplane floated on pontoons at the end of a wooden dock.

Tyrone brought the canoe in beside it and leapt out. He reached down to help Marla. She fell against Tyrone and hugged him tightly.

"What is happening to us?" she demanded, her voice drawn with fear.

Tyrone held her. "Look, wendigo madness isn't just some mental disease like the Mounties say it is. It's a lot weirder than that."

She looked up at him steadily. "The wen—"

Tyrone put his fingers on her lips. Marla was silent. He took his fingers away and kissed her instead. For a second it shocked her, but then she realized it was exactly what she wanted.

Tyrone stood back with his hands on each of her

shoulders. "After we talk to the police, I want you to go back to the Keewatin and wait for me there. Do you promise?"

Marla nodded. "I'll wait." She sniffled and wiped tears from the corners of her eyes. Arm in arm they walked up the dock to a frame cabin. An RCMP sign hung beside the door.

The lone constable on duty, a man named Brown, listened carefully to Tyrone. He was a short, slightly plump man with sharp, no-nonsense eyes. Tyrone gave him only the barest details. Mark had gone berserk. Kyla had disappeared.

He had barely finished, when two officers arrived to start a new shift. Constable Brown phoned for reinforcements from a nearby detachment. He turned on an air horn mounted outside the cabin door. The shrill whoops cut the morning stillness and echoed over the settlement. Then he went back inside and unlocked a cabinet full of guns.

A few minutes later a dozen men from the settlement crowded into the office. They had dressed hastily, some wearing jackets over pajama tops, their boot laces still untied. Two, both native men, exchanged dark glances during Constable Brown's briefing.

"Joe and Pierre Bluefish are fishing out there," one announced tersely.

"On the other side of the peninsula from us," Tyrone interjected. "We saw their camp yesterday."

The constable handed out shotguns from the cabinet. Tyrone swallowed. Those deadly weapons were going to be used to kill his best friend. He remembered the crystals of red ice that fell from Mark's wounds. Mark was frozen inside. He had called a wendigo, and a wendigo had come. Now Mark was one of them.

Tyrone's best friend had become a monster. He telephoned the Keewatin and spoke to his mother, telling her only that Kyla and Mark were lost in the wilderness. Then he arranged for a car to drive to the settlement to pick up Marla.

Soon Tyrone was ripping across Lake of the Woods on a speedboat, leading the policemen back to the campsite. The men from the settlement followed in three more boats. A strong wind had blown up from the northwest, covering the sky with a bank of thick gray clouds that hid the sun. As they neared the peninsula, one of the boats headed for the fishing camp on the other side.

When Tyrone reached the campsite, a scene of stupendous destruction met his eyes. Mark had come back. The canoe had been hacked to pieces, the tents ripped and torn, the cooler and lanterns smashed, clothing and equipment thrown helter-skelter.

Several men began searching the perimeter of the forest. The human arm was gone, but a trail of blood on leaves and tree branches led into the forest, toward the center of the peninsula.

Before Constable Brown could order a further search, the last boat raced around the tip of the peninsula. As it slowed and approached the shore, Tyrone saw grim faces on the four men aboard. The driver cut the engine in shallow water. Two men jumped out and waded ashore.

"Both dead," one said bleakly. He drew the side of his hand along his neck, his shoulders. "Cut to pieces."

The other man began speaking angrily in a native dialect.

"Slow down, slow down!" Constable Brown ordered. "I can understand if you speak slowly."

One of the natives spoke again, this time with the RCMP officer listening carefully. When the man had finished, Brown stood with his arms akimbo, an expression of pique on his face.

"What's happening?" Tyrone demanded.

"They refuse to go into the woods to look for your friends. We'll have to get searchers from another settlement, fifty miles from here." The Mountie shook his head in exasperation. "They're superstitious. They say a wendigo is on the loose."

Marla waited at the Keewatin. At noon she telephoned Kyla's parents in New York, telling them that Kyla was missing, and they were searching the forest. Mr. Recki announced he was heading up to Kenora immediately. Then she called home. The phone at her parents' New York apartment rang once. Before it was answered, she set down the receiver. Instead, she pulled an armchair up to the window that overlooked the lake. She waited, numb, staring outside and hoping Tyrone would return soon.

She wanted to tell him about her nightly aerial trips across the star-filled heavens. They were not just dreams. She had called the wendigo's name, and now it came for her, just as it had come for Mark. For the last few days her eyes had been bloodshot, and sunlight sometimes seemed blindingly bright. Were these signs of her impending transformation? Would she become like Mark? She wrapped her arms around her body and it was still warm. Her heart pounded in her chest, not yet frozen. Marla remembered the sweet contentedness she felt in her flights across the northern skies, ice cold, yet oblivious of pain. Terrified, but enraptured in the arms of a monster. Mark had sunk into bloodthirsty depravity. What did the wendigo want from her? And if she told Tyrone, would she lose him too?

It was almost evening when Tyrone returned to the Keewatin. Marla rose when he entered her room. She fell into his arms.

"Well, good news and bad," he said gently, hugging her.

"Just say it," Marla told him, looking at him steadily.

Tyrone spoke in a voice that was almost inaudible. "We haven't been able to find any trace of Kyla."

Marla felt as if she'd been hit by a fist. She felt her legs tremble. Tyrone held her tightly. "No, don't you see, Marla. *No trace.* Mark killed the two fishermen we saw on the other side of the peninsula, and left a trail of blood through the woods to our campsite. It wasn't Kyla's blood. I don't think Mark killed her. She's out there somewhere. She's lost. But I'm sure she's still alive."

Kyla had refused to panic. She spent the night on a low branch of a huge old pine tree, nodding off toward dawn despite the cold. She awoke with the branch digging into her spine. The darkness of night had ebbed, and the forest was a ghostly gray.

Her first thought was that by then—or at least very soon—Tyrone and Marla would discover her missing and look for her. She jumped down from the tree and stretched her aching body. Then she looked up through the canopy of branches and needles, trying to see where the sun was in the east. The sky was completely overcast with a sullen layer of gray clouds that diffused the light almost completely. They had watched the sun go down over the lake the night before. Assuming she had walked inland off the peninsula, Kyla decided the lake was to her right, and set off.

She hiked through a landscape in which slopes of rock alternated with thick stands of spruce. She felt as if she were climbing, which was discomfiting. She didn't remember walking downhill the night before. Gradually the cloud cover brightened as the sun rose higher, but it wasn't until midmorning that Kyla could discern its hazy white disk behind the overcast sky.

She realized she was going ninety degrees the wrong way, probably walking parallel to the shoreline instead of toward it. She changed direction, and soon found herself circling an enormous swamp that had drowned a vast stretch of forest. At first she thought surely she had reached low-lying land near the lakeshore, and it raised her hopes. But after walking more than an hour, sometimes sinking into soggy wet ground and having to retreat, it was late afternoon and the lake was nowhere in sight.

Hunger gnawed at her stomach, and her throat was parched. The white disk of sun was gone, obscured by cloud cover that became darker every second. The drowned forest was endless. The wind picked up, and Kyla felt raindrops splatter against her face. They trickled along her cheeks like tears.

The prevailing winds in the north at this time of year came from the northwest. The wind blew from across the swamp, and by her calculations, the lake was west. She decided to continue in that direction. She came across a bed of fiddleheads—tiny ferns poking their heads from wet black soil at the edge of swamp. She knew they were edible—a springtime delicacy—and feasted on the tiny shoots. It barely sated the craving in her stomach. The water from the swamp tasted brackish and metallic, although not at all bad. She sipped at it carefully, afraid of microbes, drinking only enough to slake her thirst.

Daylight finally began to seep away in the long, lingering twilight of the north. Kyla had turned back into the forest, and was standing on a rocky slope surrounded by evergreens and thatches of shoulder-high shrubs. The twilight thickened, bleeding colors away, leaving shadows to slowly envelope her. *I should find a place to sleep,* she thought. *I'll make a bed of pine boughs.* Her inner voice was calm, but she was aware that just beneath it was a terrible realization.

The northern forest was a labyrinth that went on forever, and there was no way out. Her heart pounded. It felt as if a band were being tightened around her chest. Her lungs heaved for air, and panic rose in her throat. Kyla squatted, hugging her knees to her chest. For the first time, it occurred to her that she would die in the northern forest, lost and alone. To human eyes Kyla had disappeared from the face of the earth, and would never be seen again.

CHAPTER 16

Marla couldn't bring herself to tell Tyrone about her dreams. She knew that part of her reluctance was fear—that he would turn his back on her. But as she learned from him that Kyla had not been found by the searchers, she silently formulated a plan. She had to keep her secret from Tyrone one more night. Two days ago Kyla had told Marla that she had enormous willpower and determination, she only had to use these qualities in positive ways. Marla had thought of a way. But could she bargain with a wendigo?

She went to bed, leaving the windows wide open, the curtains swaying in the cold night air. She heaped an extra blanket over the bed, crawled between the covers, and pulled them up around her. She sank almost immediately into a heavy sleep.

Once again she began to dream.

She saw a vortex of glittering snow dancing in her room like a tiny cyclone, swirling between the bed and window. It began to take the shape of a man, transparent at first. It was who she expected—the shimmering image of Father Francis. She threw back the covers. It drew her from the bed.

"You are a wendigo," she confronted him, gazing fearlessly at his terrible bloody eyes. "Not a priest."

It stared back at her, its eyes penetrating hers. Images of the tattered mission, alcoholics and the homeless, the derelicts of society, began to fill Marla's head.

They hunger for everything, it told her without speaking. *They are filled with hunger.*

Now Marla knew that the wendigo fed there, growing stronger from the bottomless needs of desperate people. The wendigo's voice whispered inside her head like a cool, gentle wind blowing through pine boughs, soothing her with a numbing coolness.

Tonight we will see such beautiful things.

What? she demanded in her thoughts.

It answered immediately with a thought of its own. *The golden city.*

Faintly, Marla heard the rhythmic sound of children singing, like a memory spun from a faraway time. "She is beautiful, she is pretty—" It made her recall sunlight and warmth.

Father Francis began to shift and change again. He grew translucent, then larger. Antlers began to sprout from his head. Marla felt herself drawn forward, into the center of an icy mist. A huge and hairy arm wrapped itself around her like a cape.

Instantly she was flying, out the window and over the vast northern forests, impervious to the cold. Below, endless evergreens stretched to a black and cloudless arctic horizon. The aurora borealis flickered in a yellow electrical arc across the north pole. They descended to the shore of a vast body of water. The wendigo touched down with one foot on a narrow gravel beach, and leapt into the sky.

They flew at tremendous speed over a dark metallic sea, storm-pitched and cold. Icebergs gathered in a flotilla. From her great height Marla saw an island of ice and tundra rise above the water, and on it, tiny from the distance, the shapes of other wendigos striding across the glacial landscape. She closed her eyes, sure she was dreaming, struggling to awaken.

What do you want from me? Marla demanded.

Again the wendigo's thoughts infiltrated her own. As if looking through a window onto the past, she saw Father Francis staring at her face on the cover of a magazine, the wendigo's flight to New York City on the winds of the mysterious late-spring blizzard. She saw him watching her, following her down the snow-encrusted city streets. She felt an immense starvation roiling in the monster's belly, and where the heart was, for just a moment, a monumental longing. Then an icy numbness. The creature answered. *To be with you.*

Fear rose from Marla's gut and caught in her throat. She thought, *I'll become a cannibal!*

We will be wendigos forever! it answered quickly.

Marla was aware of the approach of a deafening noise. *No! First you must take me to find Kyla!* she demanded, willing it as clearly as she could. There was a sudden stillness in her head. She had the sensation of a tiny surprised question, shyly asked.

Why?

Because I love her. Because she's my friend. Grief and fear welled up inside Marla, all the anguish and worry that underlay her plea. The wendigo understood need. *I need to.*

The golden city? it thought, tempting Marla again.

She felt the strange, cold peace percolate through her body. She felt content. She heard children singing. She wanted to see the golden city. But she forced herself to long for Kyla again, and with all her will she commanded the wendigo: *Tonight find Kyla. Tomorrow I will see the golden city.*

She felt the massive hairy arms tighten around her, pushing the air from her lungs, squeezing her, crushing her. When she opened her eyes, she was skimming above a landscape of forest, dotted with thousands of lakes.

Suddenly her speed slowed, and she fell quickly toward the forest. The tips of fir trees came at her. She was hovering a dozen feet above the ground. Below her Kyla lay, dirty and bedraggled, sound asleep on a bed of pine boughs.

Kyla woke up. Her eyes opened and she was instantly alert. She felt an immediate presence somewhere overhead. In a tree, she thought. An animal or a bird. She was completely cold, and shivered violently. Then she heard something else deep in the forest. It was the sound of voices chanting, and drums beating like a human heart.

She tried to get up, sore and dizzy, too cold to move, but forced herself, still not sure if she was dreaming, or, worse, hallucinating. She caught her balance, and searched the gloom for movement or animal eyes. There was none. The faraway chanting rose higher and then faded in an even rhythm, with the ever-present drum keeping time.

People, she thought. It was a word that meant one thing: rescue. She could barely see in the dark, but holding her arms ahead of her, she groped between trees in the direction of the noise. She saw an orange glow far ahead, flickering between trees. As she went closer, the light transformed the forest into a land of shuffling shadows. Something warned her not to go any farther. She gazed from behind a tree at the edge of the woods.

The forest ended in a gravel clearing. A dozen or more native men stood in a circle around a fire. The flames illuminated several parked vehicles, a battered pickup truck and the same old Buick that had driven by the settlement store. Four men pounded wooden drums in a rhythmic beat that grew steadily faster. Not far away was an enormous pile of logs, carefully stacked. The night air was pungent with the smell of kerosene.

White Eagle, the old man whom they had seen in the canoe at Red Hawk Lake, stood before the fire, his face a ruddy red in the glow, and his long gray hair burnished orange. Two men forced a prisoner forward, his hands bound in front of him. He had high cheekbones and a broad, wide face, sad eyes, and long black hair that glistened in the firelight. For the second time, Kyla recognized the face.

It was Willie Beaver.

As Kyla watched, the wendigo fell to his knees. White Eagle raised his arms, his hands open. The two guards wrapped a cord around the prisoner's throat, crossing the ends at the back of his neck. Each held an end. They took up positions on either side, and began to pull it tight.

Kyla watched the murderer sag and shake violently. The executioners' faces grew red with strain, and the muscles on their arms tightened. The chanting rose in intensity, blending with the pounding drums. The prisoner stiffened, his body jerked violently, and finally fell limp.

Abruptly, the chanting stopped. So did the drumming. The forest was quiet except for the dull roar of the flames and the crackle of burning logs. Sparks danced in the heat waves above the fire. The executioners lowered the dead man's body to the ground. White Eagle stepped forward, dipped his hand into a leather pouch, and sprinkled the body with something.

Softly, the drumming started again, this time slow and methodical. Four men came forward and quickly wrapped the body in a burlap sheet. Another man began pouring a golden liquid over it. White Eagle pulled a burning stick from the fire and held it aloft. The other natives lifted the dead man's body and carried it toward the stacked logs. With a great heave they threw it on top.

For a moment the body lay still. Suddenly, it began to move, as if the shrouded corpse were struggling to get free! The natives fell back, one moaning with fear, another shielding his eyes. White Eagle stepped forward and threw the burning brand onto the stack of logs. With a loud whoosh it burst into flames.

A terrible scream broke from the body on the pyre as the burlap caught. The corpse doubled up and fell back, twisting and writhing. Slowly, its movements began to weaken. Burning logs crashed, unleashing a whirlwind of glowing sparks that spiraled toward the black sky. Finally, the corpse was still, a blackened husk burning fiercely amid the flames.

Kyla snapped. She belted into the forest, running blindly, not caring about the noise, the direction, the branches that smashed into her face, the crevasses between the rocks that caught her feet, the skin scraped from her face and hands when she fell. Finally she stopped and listened carefully. She heard nothing but her own exhausted panting. No one was following. The forest was dark.

Kyla's feet and legs were wet and ice-cold. She was standing in water up to her knees. Without even starlight the night was pitch-black, yet she could make out the gaunt black of naked limbs and dead trees. Logs, fallen helter-skelter and peeled of their bark, were tangled around her like piles of bleached bones. She was lost in the immense old swamp.

She started sobbing and shivering at the same time, the ice-cold water sapping her strength. She struggled, moving step by step, testing the water for depth and trying in vain to see where the forest was, where solid ground began, reaching for a dead limb to pull her from the muck.

She heard the low whistle of wind. It grew louder until it was almost deafening. Kyla looked up. Something flashed overhead. She screamed. The dead limb snapped. Kyla fell back. Suddenly she felt massive arms grip her waist and lift her into the air!

She was dreaming, she told herself, or dying. She was soaring across water, just above the furrowed waves, crossing Lake of the Woods at a tremendous speed with the first white light of dawn barely a crack on the eastern horizon and the streetlights of Kenora twinkling on the approaching shore.

She turned to look at the face of the creature who carried her, and saw a man with a small round head, and smooth skin, scarred around the lips as if he had been burned in a horrible fire. She turned her head the other way. She was looking at Marla.

* * *

Tyrone was up at the crack of dawn, emerging from the cabin as the eastern sky took on a rosy glow. He glanced up. The wind had changed direction and the sky was clearing. He hurried toward the Jeep, eager to join the search parties that would be setting out within the hour.

As he drove along the road toward the Keewatin, he noticed a low-lying mist over the lake, drifting among the boats and obscuring the end of the dock. The white air swirled and parted. Kyla stood alone on the narrow beach.

Tyrone turned the steering wheel, and the Jeep bounced down the slope onto a gravel service road. He jumped out, his nostrils assailed by the pungent odor of dank, decaying vegetation.

"Kyla!" He said her name half with fear and half with astonishment. She was soaking wet, covered with dead leaves and mud, her blond hair plastered down across her face. She was shivering from exposure, and her eyes were vacant.

"Where in hell did you come from?" he asked her, glancing around. Quickly he slipped off his jacket and slung it around her shoulders. She didn't acknowledge him. Her eyes stared into space, and her mouth hung slightly open. Her skin was blue from cold.

Suddenly Tyrone heard footsteps crunching into the sand. He turned just as Marla materialized from the mist. She wore only a robe over her long, thin nightgown, and her hair was mussed and wild. Her eyes met Tyrone's, but she walked directly to Kyla and took her in her arms. Kyla shrank against her, and clung silently.

Marla looked at Tyrone again, warning him off. Without a word she led Kyla slowly toward the great log hotel that loomed above them.

Tyrone waited on the beach while the mist shifted around them. When they were gone, he looked around, peering carefully at the sand where the water lapped against the shore. Finally he found what he was looking for, already half dissolved by the waves. It was a giant footprint with a single great toe, pressed deeply into the sand and perfectly formed.

CHAPTER 17

The Kenora Hospital was a modern low-rise with long, fluorescent-lit corridors of soft blue walls and gleaming white tile trim.

An ambulance took Kyla there shortly after Tyrone found her. He drove Marla to the hospital behind it. Sergeant Clarkson, the same RCMP officer who had come to see them after the discovery of Sylvain's frozen body, was waiting at the emergency room entrance. They were shown into a small, private lounge next to the hospital's chapel.

Clarkson pulled his notebook from a jacket pocket and looked from Tyrone to Marla, his cool blue eyes loaded with skepticism. "It's more than fifty miles as the crow flies from where she disappeared," he said slowly. "Longer by road. So how'd she get to the lakeshore outside the Keewatin."

"Why don't you explain it," Tyrone said, barely hid-ing the insolence in his voice. "Last time you guys had all the answers."

"I thought you might be able to throw some light on it," Clarkson said coolly.

Tyrone looked at Marla strangely. He shrugged. "Beats me," he said. "All I know is that she disappeared two nights ago when we were camping."

"What about Mark?" Marla interjected abruptly. "Have you found him?"

Clarkson paused a moment, staring again at the two teenagers, his pen poised over a page in his notebook. He seemed to be doing a mental assessment of them. Finally he shook his head. "Not a clue. It's as if he disappeared from the face of the earth. We'll keep looking though. As long as we have warrants for his arrest for killing those two native men, we'll keep looking."

There was a light tap on the door of the small room. It opened and a white-coated doctor stepped halfway into the room. He glanced at Marla and Tyrone, casting them a reassuring smile.

"Your friend has suffered from severe exposure and shock," he told them. "We've listed her in serious but stable condition. She's sleeping now. She'll be fine."

Marla heaved a huge sigh and looked at Tyrone, whose face also showed relief. Sergeant Clarkson jotted something down in his notebook.

"Your friend's parents are coming for her?" he asked.

Marla nodded. "Her father's flying up from New York today."

The RCMP officer flipped his notebook closed and stuffed it back into his pocket. "Don't leave Kenora without letting me know," he said in a tone that carried a warning.

* * *

Although the doctor told them that Kyla might sleep for several days, Marla insisted on staying at the hospital. Tyrone waited with her. They went to the cafeteria for lunch and afterward took a walk across the spacious lawns that surrounded the low-rise modern hospital.

The air was limp, the sky bleeding white from a thin high-altitude haze. The grounds had been landscaped with copses of white birch, but as usual the real forest was visible on one side, opposite the service road that led behind the hospital. A long silence reigned between them, one that promised the inevitable conversation they both dreaded. Marla spoke first.

"What happened to Mark?" She glanced sideways at Tyrone.

The Canadian teenager quickly shrugged. "I don't know exactly. I mean, he's a showoff. Kind of power hungry, and always trying to rule the scene. It was like that when I spent that year in California. And sometimes, if you didn't do what he wanted, he could get real ugly about it. I always kind of ignored it, because it didn't seem worth getting heated up about. But now it's like all that just took over his personality, and turned him into this . . . this . . ."

"Monster," said Marla quietly. She looked up at Tyrone. "A wendigo."

"That night around the campfire—your first night here, remember—he stood up and yelled for the wendigo to come."

"And the very next day Mark led us to Sylvain's frozen body," Marla reflected.

"Maybe Mark knew it was there." Tyrone nodded slowly. "The wendigo must have showed it to him after it possessed Mark."

"Remember how pale he suddenly looked? Wearing sunglasses. And that's when he started beating Kyla at tennis," Marla said suddenly in realization. "She kept saying how fast he moved." She shuddered with the memory of Mark appearing out of nowhere in the hotel corridor when he made his pass at her, the icy coldness of his body and his lips.

"He started taking on the creature's powers."

"But how?" Marla demanded. "It's all supposed to be just a legend, a fairy tale!"

Tyrone exhaled a deep breath of air. "The legend of the wendigo is about hunger. Starvation. For thousands of years the native people had to face starvation if the winter was too long, or if the animal population fell. When it was real bad, they survived by eating the bodies of the dead. Cannibalism. So they made up a story about a cannibal monster to represent hunger. Maybe if enough people believe in something long enough, it comes true. The reality is that wendigos aren't hungry just for food. They have a deep, bottomless hunger that can never be satisfied. And one of them keeps coming back to the Keewatin for its victims. Mark hungered for power, and he got it."

"But what a price to pay. A heart of ice." Marla looked at Tyrone. "What should we do?"

"Wendigos must be killed," he said firmly, staring at the edge of the forest. "They must be killed."

An uncomfortable silence settled between them, as if both knew the question that lingered like an intrusive guest. This time Tyrone spoke first.

"How did you know Kyla was there? I mean, at the lakeshore this morning at five-thirty?"

Marla looked at him quickly, turned, and slowly

walked a few steps away. "It was a dream. Sort of." She stopped and swung around to face him.

Tyrone turned pale, and stared at her.

"I've been . . . dreaming. At night. Since I came here."

He stepped toward Marla and grabbed her, his hands locking onto her arms. Her skin was warm. "What have you been dreaming?"

"That I've been flying." Marla shrank from his reaction. "At night. Over the forest." She pulled Tyrone's hands away from her arms. "Flying over the earth with the forest below me, and lakes and more forest ahead of me as far as the eye can see."

She laughed a little and looked quickly away, gazing across the rolling lawns and birch trees to the great green forest beyond. "I like the dreams. Am I turning into a wendigo, Tyrone?"

He looked at her steadily. "I don't know, Marla."

She stared at him, unable to read the strange expression on his face. "How will I stop it?"

"Stop giving it what it wants."

"What does it want?"

"I don't know, Marla. Maybe you should ask what *you* want."

It was already early afternoon. They walked back to the hospital in silence, each of them pondering their conversation. Marla was scared. She'd told Tyrone only part of the story, and already she sensed a distance from him. How could she tell him the whole thing—that she'd bargained with the wendigo. And that she wasn't just dreaming.

Inside, they waited again at the door to Kyla's room, sitting stiffly in metal and plastic chairs next to a coffee table covered with frayed and ancient magazines. Two policemen lounged at the end of the corridor, guarding access like mythical griffins. Several local reporters and photographers had appeared, but were quickly turned away.

Shortly after they got back, there was a sudden bustle of activity, with nurses and orderlies going in and out the door of Kyla's room. Soon a doctor arrived and disappeared inside. He emerged a few minutes later and beamed at Marla and Tyrone.

"Your friend's awake," he announced. "She wants to see you. For just a minute."

Kyla lay in bed, her face wan and her long blond hair splayed across the pillow. A clear plastic oxygen tube led from an outlet on the wall behind the bed to a loop around her head and into her nose. Marla sat in the chair beside the bed and took Kyla's hand in hers. Tyrone hung back, several feet from the bed.

Kyla smiled weakly. "They've stuck so many needles into me, I can barely move," she said softly, trying to laugh a little.

"Oh, Kyla," Marla said, her eyes brimming with tears. "I was afraid I'd never see you again."

"I was afraid I'd never see *anyone* again." Kyla glanced at Tyrone. "They told me you found me outside the hotel."

Tyrone walked closer. "How did you get back to the Keewatin, Kyla?"

Kyla shifted uncomfortably and turned her head sideways on the pillow, facing away from her friends.

"It was more than fifty miles from where you got lost," Tyrone persisted. "You had to cross roads and highways—someone would have found you before you got there."

"I don't know!" Kyla tried to shout but could not summon the energy, and her words came out as a hoarse whisper. She flung her head around to face Marla and Tyrone. "I don't know," she repeated softly. "I was lost, and I saw . . . I saw . . ." Her blue eyes clouded with terror as her mind's eye framed the burning pyre and the body thrown upon it. Kyla sank back into her pillow. "I was flying," she said in an almost dreamlike manner. "Over the lake. I was coming home."

"How, Kyla?" Tyrone asked quietly. "How were you flying?"

She looked up at Marla. "Someone came to get me. And when I looked, I saw you."

Marla stood. She noticed Tyrone staring at her, and she looked nervously away. She began to speak in a monotone, almost like a chant. "He was in New York, you know, that day when winter came. He followed me. I wasn't going crazy after all."

Marla walked several feet away and slowly turned to them. Her face was almost expressionless. "He comes to me at night when I'm dreaming. It's as if he swallows my mind and I exist inside him, hearing his thoughts as if he's talking to me."

Tyrone stared at her, resisting the impulse to back away. Marla's eyes were empty, or fixed upon a distant spot in some other, unimaginable universe.

"He leaps from the windowsill of my room at the Keewatin and then we fly out into the night, where the darkness is like soup and the stars are chunks of brittle ice. We fly over forests and lakes that go on forever and ever. I think the entire earth is forest and lake. Last night, though, I wasn't dreaming. He wanted to take me somewhere, but I made him find Kyla instead."

"It!" Tyrone said angrily. "It's not a he, Marla. It's a thing!"

Marla came back into present time. Her eyes flickered toward Tyrone. She shivered, and wrapped her arms around her body. "I always feel so cold."

She stared at Kyla. Kyla returned her gaze, hanging on to Marla's next words, somehow knowing what she was about to say before the words were even spoken.

"You were sleeping on a bed of pine boughs in the forest," Marla told her. "I was looking down at you. He wouldn't go closer. I heard a drum beating somewhere. You woke up and started running through the trees. He followed you until you saw the fire burning in the woods, and the men—"

"Stop it!" Kyla tried to shout, struggling to sit up in bed and tearing at the oxygen tube below her nose.

Tyrone rushed to the bed and put his arms around her. He turned to face Marla. "What men?" he demanded.

Marla gazed at him without speaking.

Instead, Kyla began to speak. "Native men. White Eagle was there. And the man on the wanted poster at the store. Willie Beaver. They strangled him and threw his body on the fire."

"You started running through the forest and you went into the swamp." Marla walked toward the bed, staring at Kyla, her voice almost a whisper now. "And then we were flying again. Together. Across the lake." She looked at Tyrone. "I woke up in bed at the Keewatin. The windows were wide open, and there was a horrible smell in the room. But I knew where Kyla was. I went down to the lake to get her. I just did it."

"It's trying to possess you, Marla!" Tyrone said. "The same way it possessed Mark!"

"But it's not filled with hatred or blood lust. It's not like what's happened to Mark!" Marla protested. Her voice dropped. "All I feel from it is this ravenous hunger, it's like, inexhaustible. This incredible emptiness that has to be filled, but with something greater than just food or power. It's . . . it's like it wants to be loved."

"Tyrone's right. It's bewitching you!" Kyla murmured coldly. "It's an evil creature, a cannibal monster! You want to have a heart of ice, Marla? You want to be dead inside?"

"It saved your life!" Marla protested.

"*You* saved my life," Kyla shot back. Her head sagged and she closed her eyes. "I have to sleep," she murmured. "You have to go."

CHAPTER 18

Marla and Tyrone climbed into the Jeep, and Tyrone drove down to the main road. Instead of turning left, which led back to the Keewatin, he turned right and accelerated.

"Where are we going?" Marla said sharply.

Tyrone kept his eyes on the highway, and was silent for a moment. He reached across the seat, his hand falling on hers, and resting there, warm and strong. He looked at her.

"Can you trust me?"

Marla looked at Tyrone as he turned back to watch the road. The answer came from deep inside her, like a cork floating to the surface of water. She had no doubts at all. She nodded. "Yes."

Tyrone shifted into a higher gear. In a moment they were traveling quickly along the narrow blacktop, leaving behind the cabins and trailer parks that crowded Kenora's outskirts, and heading into the wilderness.

Once again the vast primeval forest crowded in on each side of the road. The sky had cleared, and the late afternoon sun baked the windshield. Marla rolled her window down, feeling the cool fresh air bathe her skin, her long hair fluttering behind her in the wind.

After twenty minutes Tyrone turned onto a gravel road. Marla recognized it as the same one they had taken on their camping trip. She rolled up her window to keep the dust out, and soon the air inside was stifling. They passed the settlement store, but instead of turning into the forest as they had before, Tyrone steered the Jeep straight ahead, in the direction of the Ojibway reservation. Fifteen minutes later he braked and swung the Jeep onto a dirt track that disappeared into the forest.

The Jeep bucked and climbed over ruts and potholes, trembling violently as it rumbled over rain-carved ridges, almost shaking Marla's teeth out. They climbed a hill and lumbered down the other side, passing the edge of a great swamp, where the skeletal trunks of dead trees stood like silent sentinels. The dirt trail had softened, and the ride became smoother. The fir trees were replaced by a forest of tall, spindly aspens with leaves that flickered like pale green sequins in the breeze. Ahead of them was a clearing. Marla shuddered. She knew exactly where they were.

The Jeep rolled to a stop. Tyrone turned off the engine.

Marla made no effort to leave her seat. "I don't want to go out there," she snapped.

"Suit yourself." Tyrone eyed her, then glanced away. He opened his door and stepped out, slamming it shut behind him.

Marla closed her eyes and remained motionless,

summoning up the courage to follow. When she opened them, she saw Tyrone through the windshield, walking toward the remains of a bonfire in the center of the clearing. She took a deep breath and reached for the door handle.

"How did you know it was here?" she asked, stepping outside. The cool air hit her, spreading from the forest shade that surrounded them, despite the sunlight filtering through the canopy of aspen leaves. In mud near the Jeep she saw the deep ruts made by car tires the night before. The pyre had burned down to almost nothing, little more than a pile of ash and charred, blackened logs. Slowly, Marla walked over to where Tyrone stood, staring at the remains of the fire. She repeated her question.

"I knew it had to be near the Ojibway reservation. When Kyla told us about being lost, she said she tried to head west along the lake, but went inland instead and got lost in a great swamp."

He looked around on the ground and finally stalked to the edge of the forest. A moment later he returned with a long, thick stick. He started poking at the ashes, pushing aside the remnants of blackened logs.

"What are you looking for?" Marla demanded, shivering and wishing they would leave the place.

"Bones. Even a fire this big wouldn't destroy all the bones. If we find some, it'll prove Kyla's story."

"Tyrone, we don't need to prove Kyla's story."

Tyrone kept prodding and poking, slowly circling the pile of ashes.

Marla raised her voice. "Tyrone, I was here! I saw it happen!"

A deep, solemn voice boomed from the forest. "There are no bones!"

Marla jumped, her spine rippling with terror. Tyrone spun around to face the intruder.

White Eagle walked purposefully from the edge of the forest into the clearing. The native man wore an ancient fringed jacket, and his long gray hair was held back by a red bandanna. Marla felt like an animal caught in the headlights of a speeding car. His dark eyes glittered, but his face was expressionless. He stopped six feet from them.

"You're a shaman," Tyrone said, staring at White Eagle. "A medicine man."

"In my people's tongue, I am a *ma-mandowin-ninih*. To you, a medicine man. Or a sorcerer." He pointed to the remains of the fire. "You will find no bones. The skeleton was ice. After the flesh burned away, it melted in the flames."

Marla suppressed a cry, an urge to run into the forest and far away. Like a film loop in her mind's eye, she saw the flickering firelight, a man with a leather thong around his neck, his tongue lolling from his mouth, eyes bulging, and the face of White Eagle overseeing the execution. She grabbed Tyrone, her fingers clutching his arm. Tyrone stepped in front of her, facing White Eagle.

"He submitted to death," White Eagle stated flatly, his glittering eyes on Marla. "He asked to die. It is our people's custom. He was becoming a wendigo, and he had tasted human flesh. He knew that he would crave it again."

"It was horrible!" Marla cried.

"No more horrible than the beast that Willie Beaver saw," the native sorcerer replied evenly. His dark eyes probed hers. "At the Keewatin, the ground is soaked with the blood of this wendigo's victims. My ancestors, who built a village there, were tricked by it, and hungered for food. Wendigos feed on hunger, and this one grew bigger until it destroyed them. Then fur traders came. They hungered, not for food, but for wealth, and this wendigo grew strong again. It returns to the Keewatin because it can still smell blood. This wendigo is very old and very powerful. Willie Beaver and Sylvain Charbadeau saw it, and I think your friend has seen it too."

White Eagle raised his head. His nostrils flared as if he'd caught a scent on a stray current of air. He pointed at her.

"You smell of moss." The native sorcerer looked disdainful. "Have you tasted human flesh?" He sniffed at the air and shook his head. "No," he concluded. "Not yet."

Marla moved out from behind Tyrone. She walked closer to White Eagle and faced him squarely. "I've been dreaming—he—it comes at night and I start to dream—"

Marla's chest began to heave, and suddenly her eyes were filled with tears. An immense quantity of sorrow welled up inside her. She put her hand to her mouth to stifle a sob. In a step Tyrone was beside her, his arm reaching around her shoulder, pulling her close.

"What is it *doing* to me?" Marla implored, resisting Tyrone and looking at White Eagle. "It—it *wants* me for some reason."

"It has not possessed you yet," White Eagle said quietly, still without a flicker of emotion. "You must decide."

"Decide what?" she demanded.

White Eagle stared at her. "If you will fight this creature off. Or if you will have a heart of ice." The *ma-*

mandowin-ninih turned and began to walk toward an old pickup parked in the shadow of an immense pine tree.

Marla pulled from Tyrone and ran after him. "I'm going home," she announced loudly. "I'm going back to New York tomorrow."

White Eagle stopped at the door to the pickup truck. "It will follow," he said without turning. "Keewatin is lord of the north wind. Where Keewatin blows, the wendigo goes too."

"But I know who the wendigo is!" Marla said suddenly. White Eagle stared hard at her. There was a moment of silence.

"He's changed his shape so he can live among people." Marla looked nervously from White Eagle to Tyrone. Quickly, she told them about the strange priest who called himself Father Francis.

Tyrone looked doubtful. "Why would a wendigo live like that?"

"It has chosen to live among desperate people," White Eagle said. "It feeds on their need."

"Then we have to destroy it!" Tyrone said loudly. "Before it destroys someone else the way it's destroyed Mark."

Calmly, White Eagle climbed into the driver's seat. He stared straight ahead through the windshield. "It is very difficult to kill a wendigo. Wendigos are strong. Perhaps a wendigo can kill a wendigo, but I do not think a man can, no matter how brave."

Marla ran to the open window. "But Willie Beaver was a wendigo! And you, he—" She motioned toward the pile of ashes and charred logs in the middle of the clearing.

"He submitted willingly. It is our people's custom."

"But you destroyed him!" Marla pointed out.

"The wendigo's heart and skeleton are of ice. The heat of a fire melts ice. But wendigos are very clever, and do not go near fire."

White Eagle turned the key in the ignition, and the engine sprang to life. He slipped it in gear. The pickup edged forward.

"What will I do?" Marla demanded. There was an edge of panic to her voice. "How can I stop it?"

White Eagle braked and turned to look at her. Again his dark eyes bored into hers, while his face remained without visible emotion. "You must stop being hungry," the sorcerer told her.

The engine revved, and the pickup surged forward. It disappeared up the narrow dirt road, leaving a long, thick cloud of dust snaking in its wake.

They drove back to the Keewatin Lodge. The sun was setting, rimming the western sky purple and red, transforming the trees at the edge of the forest into gaunt twilight silhouettes. For a long time they rode in silence. Tyrone broke it by speaking first.

"You okay?" he asked.

"I don't know," Marla said, searching for a better answer and coming up empty. "What did he mean, that I have to stop being hungry?"

Tyrone thought a moment before answering. "The wendigo feeds off our longing, and grows stronger until it destroys us. So if you want to stop it, you have to stop wanting whatever it is that—"

"But how!" Marla interrupted impatiently.

"What do you want?" Tyrone challenged her. "More than anything."

It was a question she'd asked herself a lot. To be

filled, Marla knew, was the quick answer. Filled up, so the empty space at the center of her soul was gone. In the shadowy interior of a car hurtling down a highway at dusk with Tyrone at the wheel, the glowing lights of the instrument panel, the blast of warm air from the dashboard heater, somehow these things—and everything—made that moment intimate.

Her memory flashed through the events of the last days, and a realization came to her with total clarity: that everyone lived with the cards life dealt them, not just her. She thought of Kyla's confession that she was gay, and how she'd trusted Marla with it; she thought about her own bulimia. Suddenly she realized what she was trying to throw up—a life that had been foisted upon her, not chosen. And she remembered Kyla's advice: You've got to live your own life.

"Well?" Tyrone prodded.

At that instant Marla decided to be completely honest and say what she really felt.

"For you to love me for who I really am." Marla could scarcely believe that she was saying it out loud. It felt good. It felt real.

Tyrone reached across the seat, took her hand, and squeezed it. He was beaming. "No problem there."

They arrived at the hotel at dusk, the great log lodge rising like a medieval castle over the lake, and the lights of Kenora twinkling again on the farther shore. Overhead, stars were appearing in the inky sky. There was a message at the desk for Marla. Mr. Recki, Kyla's father, had arrived, and Tyrone's mother had accompanied him to the hospital. Tyrone glanced at his watch.

"Visiting hours there are till nine, and it's just after seven," he told her. "Do you want to drive over?"

Marla shook her head. "I'm exhausted. I need to lie down for an hour."

"Should I come for you when my mother gets back with Mr. Recki?"

Marla nodded. She walked closer to Tyrone, and stood on tiptoe to kiss him lightly on his lips.

Tyrone climbed into the Jeep, glancing quickly in the back to make sure his ax was still there. The long wooden handle had been replaced since the fight with Mark. The last glimmers of the northern twilight remained, barely a glow in the west, transforming the pine trees on the Keewatin's lawn into towering black silhouettes. The lights of Kenora glittered up the lake. Tyrone turned onto the highway in that direction and accelerated. A sudden sense of purpose made him grip the steering wheel.

He drove downtown, past the Husky the Musky monument at Harbourfront Park, into the warehouse district. He saw the orange glow of fire and a tower of thick black smoke against the evening sky even before he turned onto the block where the Mission of St. Francis was located. The street was crowded with police cars and fire engines. A knot of bystanders stood behind barricades. A cop walked in front of the Jeep with his hand up.

Tyrone pulled over to the curb and rolled down his window. "What's happening?" he shouted over the noise of sirens and the raging fire.

The policeman approached the Jeep. "Couple of winos set fire to that mission building. We nabbed them running out of there with a can of gasoline."

Tyrone gazed quickly around. Long arcs of water from high-pressure hoses poured into the conflagration. The plate-glass windows along the front were a wall of flames, and fire licked along the roof.

"You gotta turn around and back out of here," the policeman ordered.

"Did that old priest who runs the place get out?" Tyrone asked, feigning only casual interest.

"They think he's still in there." The cop sneered. "Those crazy winos said they burned him out 'cause he's a wendigo!"

Tyrone put the Jeep in reverse and backed out of the street. He had gone there to confront the priest, and to kill a wendigo if he had to. Maybe it was too late for Mark, but it wasn't for Marla—yet. It looked as if someone else had beat him to it. He cast a lingering last look. The tongues of flame that glowed and flickered against mountains of billowing black smoke looked like the fires of hell. In the group of bystanders on the corner he spotted White Eagle. The sorcerer was staring at Tyrone. He turned and disappeared into the crowd.

White Eagle's words formed in Tyrone's mind with chilling clarity. "Wendigos are very clever. They do not go near fire."

Tyrone drove back to the Keewatin and parked the Jeep by the cabin. Then he started toward the hotel. Night had fallen, and what was left of the waning moon wouldn't rise for a few hours. The sky was brilliant with stars. He picked up his pace and began to jog. As he passed the deserted tennis courts, he saw something lying in the middle of the clay, near the net.

Tyrone stopped, peering through the eerie dim light cast by the stars, trying to make out what it was. Finally he detoured, passing through a gate in the Cyclone fence around the courts, still unable to make out the large dark object. A smell assailed his nostrils, putrid and decaying, the stench of muck from the bottom of a swamp. He approached slowly. The grass was covered with cold dew, and his pants legs were wet below the knee by the time he reached the courts.

It was the carcass of a deer, its throat and belly torn open, its guts emptied, the flesh drained of blood. The animal's head was twisted at a strange angle, and its glassy eyes stared balefully into the night.

Tyrone swallowed. He looked around and overhead. The disgusting stench seemed to grow stronger. He knew this was Mark's doing—or worse, the ancient monster that had haunted the Keewatin for centuries. And Marla was alone in her room. Tyrone turned and ran for the hotel.

CHAPTER 19

In her room at the Keewatin, Marla stood before the bathroom mirror, staring at her face, the face that launched a thousand magazines. She knew that when she went back to New York she wasn't going to model anymore. She had always done it because it was what her mother wanted, and for no other reason. Now, she realized, she had to please herself first.

She had not binged on food, or thrown up, for almost three days. It wasn't long, but it was a start. It was more than just her anxiety about Kyla, her fear of the strange northern horror that had changed her. It was the message hidden between the lines of White Eagle's last words. For the first time in her life Marla had to make her own decision: to fight this horror herself, with no one's help, not even Tyrone's.

As if it had been beckoned by her thoughts, Marla felt a sudden icy breeze filter through the room. She turned around and saw it at the window, coruscating in the moonlight, a whirlwind of glittering, sparkling snow. It shifted, and began to take form. The face of Father Francis floated in the window. His arm, humongous and covered with thick hair, reached for her with waves of fathomless longing.

In the distance, as if muffled by a pillow, Marla heard heavy thuds. Someone was banging at the door of her room. It made no difference. Entranced, Marla walked toward the monster. It was ready to take her, and not just for a magical mystery tour. This time the wendigo wanted everything.

Tyrone clenched his fist and pounded hard on Marla's door. Still no answer. He grabbed the handle and shook it, banging the door with his other hand. Nothing. He stood back and kicked. The frame splintered and the door sprang open. He burst into Marla's room.

The stench of decay assailed his nostrils, almost unbearable. The bed was empty and undisturbed. A cool breeze forced its way through from the bathroom. The window was wide open. Bits of dead moss clung to the sill.

Tyrone descended the fire stairs at the end of the corridor. He exited through the emergency door onto the lawn, looking desperately in every direction for a sign of her. Shivers crawling along the back of his neck made him look overhead. The sky was brilliant with stars, the spiral arms of the Milky Way stretching across the black sky.

He raced toward the tennis courts. The deer carcass still lay there. He saw movement at the end of the court, in the darkness under a row of sixty-foot pines. Someone walked from the shadows.

"Mark?" Tyrone called out, recognizing him even in the bare luminescence from the starlight.

Mark walked closer, moving stiffly on swollen, misshapen feet. His clothes were in rags, covered with dried blood, and his red-rimmed eyes were feral. He smiled crazily at Tyrone.

"I got a friend I want you to meet! He's coming!" Mark threw his head back to the sky and howled, "Wendigoooo! Wendigoooo!"

Tyrone fled, faster than he'd ever run before. He was fifty feet from the cabin when a strange chill made him look back. Barely thirty feet behind him, Mark landed on a single leg and leapt again, bounding high into the air.

Tyrone's breath seared his lungs. He was at the Jeep. The ax lay on the seat. He dove for it. His hands closed around the wooden shaft and he swung around.

Mark landed six feet away. For the first time, Tyrone saw two long protuberances emerge from his forehead, the ends rounded and covered with fuzz. Mark was growing antlers! And his skin was covered with downy blond hair.

"C'mon, Tyrone," he shouted. "It's me, dude. Mark! Your old pal!"

"Mark, I don't want to kill you! Please!" Tyrone begged, backing away and raising the ax.

Mark laughed. Tyrone swung the ax sideways, slamming the blade against the side of Mark's head. It should have knocked him cold, even killed him. Instead, the skin split apart, and dark red ice crystals dripped down the side of Mark's face.

For a second Mark seemed dazed. The blood crystals began to move, the side of his head blurring strangely. The wound was healing almost instantly. "I'm still learning what my powers are!" he shouted gleefully. His voice was deafening.

Tyrone backed away, ready to swing the ax as hard as he had to. He made a break for it, running up the steps to the cabin's porch. The door was unlocked. He went inside and slammed it shut.

Mark leapt to the top of the steps in a single bound. He raised his foot and kicked the thick wooden door. It buckled, the window shattering. Mark walked inside. His head wound had healed completely, and yet somehow wrongly. His face was distorted, as if the bones were changing shape.

Tyrone swung the ax again, aiming the blade carefully and using all his strength. It sliced Mark's head off at the neck. His body convulsed silently, spewing red ice crystals while the head fell aside, bounced once on the floor, and lay still.

Tyrone looked at it. Mark's angry, bloodred eyes gazed up at him. They blinked! His lips opened and shut. The severed head was mouthing words! Tyrone felt a voice whispering at his ears, his movement slowing as if ice were settling into his veins. Wendigos had the power to freeze their victims. Tyrone struggled against the seeping coldness, forcing himself to avert his eyes. He turned away, and saw Mark's headless body.

Mark's arms reached out, his hands grabbing at the floor and pushing the living corpse forward. Blood crystals began to swirl around the gaping neck wound. The wendigo was a shape-shifter. It could rearrange itself—or reattach itself—at will. As Tyrone watched, Mark's body began to move, drawn toward the still-living head by some strange telepathic radar.

"No!" Tyrone screamed. He swung the ax with all his

might, driving it deep into the torso. The steel blade sank into the wooden floor. Pinned, the headless body began to squirm, the arms and legs flailing aimlessly like an overturned bug.

Tyrone had seconds to spare. He stepped gingerly around it and ran outside. A ten-gallon drum of kerosene lay on its side next to the woodpile. He turned the spigot and a stream of golden liquid spurted out. Then he wrapped his arms around the heavy steel drum and carried it into the house.

He splashed kerosene everywhere, soaking Mark's body and head. The drum of kerosene was almost empty. From far in the distance Tyrone heard a sound like the whistle of a train from hell. The nauseating stench of decay pervaded the old cabin. The sound grew louder and louder until it was deafening, painful to his eardrums. Tyrone dropped the empty drum and pressed his hand to his ears.

With a roar at the open door of the cabin, another wendigo stooped to enter, a horrible naked giant covered with fur, immense pinnacled antlers projecting from its forehead. Its eyes rolled in blood, its torn and ragged lips exposed razor-sharp teeth. It eyed Tyrone with an inhuman hatred and reached out its great, hairy arm.

Marla saw the golden city, far in the distance, at the edge of the dark globe that rolled thousands of feet below.

When she flew from the hotel window in the wendigo's arms, she closed her eyes, unable to contemplate what was happening. The cold air made her sleepy, but the monster's arms felt warm. She knew there was more than one wendigo. She'd seen, in her dreams, the island in Hudson Bay teeming with an entire race. Her wendigo was not the bloodthirsty wendigo that had haunted the land around the Keewatin for centuries, the one that had come for Willie Beaver, for Weird Sylvain, and finally for Mark.

How many were there though? The answer came easily, in a cool, persuasive voice.

Everyone has their own wendigo.

Marla heard children's voices, singing. "She is beautiful, she is pretty. She is the queen of the golden city." She opened her eyes. That was when she saw it, far across the starry night at the end of the earth, where the Canadian forest met a roiling sea flecked with ice floes. It rose on the shore, the round domes and glistening spires of a great golden city.

She heard music, a symphonic chorus of sounds that made her think, *music of the celestial spheres.* She looked down and saw marvelous wonders, as if the creature who held her had penetrated the boundary between reality and legend. Far below, the Canadian forest teemed with living spirits, and above, the northern lights were goddesses striding across the jet-black sky.

The wendigo flew on, over darkened continents whose shape she could not identify, a valley of jungle crawling with dinosaurs, cleft in a forgotten desert of white ice. Farther and farther the wendigo flew, and Marla saw the lights of fabulous cities, Atlantis and Ys, Ragnarok and Mu, glittering like jewels in their velvet darkness. Once, Marla saw another wendigo, hideously ugly, bounding great distances across the earth below.

All this, for you. The thought formed in Marla's head, and she knew it was the wendigo offering her everything. But then its insatiable longing came at her in waves, a terrible need that grew with the aching loneliness of the empty land, beyond all satisfaction, beyond a desire for Marla's beauty. It was a burning hunger for a companion, to wander perpetually the frozen reaches of the farthest skies.

Marla understood, finally, what the wendigo longed for most of all—that she become a wendigo too. She had only to take his breath into her body, icy as the arctic wind, to freeze the marrow of her bones, and turn her warm and beating heart to solid ice.

It would be wonderful, she thought, glimpsing on land far below a palace of white columns set on a mountaintop, a garden of fountains and palm trees overlooking a tropical sea. Saturn rose above the horizon, as big as the moon, with its rows of concentric rings stretched across the entire sky. The wendigo's seduction was perfect. It was a total escape. And with a frozen heart Marla knew she would cease to feel pain ever again. She would cease to feel anything.

Again the monster's ravenous hunger nudged her, this time with an insistence that left her drained.

Now?

I can't decide, thought Marla, terrified of either answer, terrified of the beast that held her, the fiery height at which they flew, miles above the turning earth. But she knew what she was thinking of—Mark, standing at the edge of the forest, a human limb hanging from his bloody hands. And Tyrone, stepping forward to protect her.

Her own longing escaped like an air bubble rising to the surface of water. Tyrone was what she wanted more than what the wendigo was offering. More than anything. And Kyla. Friends who believed in her, who loved her for who she was, and not the New York model that went only skin deep. She closed her eyes and filled her mind with a single imperative that blocked the wendigo's badgering enticements. *I want to go back. I want to see Tyrone.* She felt as if she were waking from a bad dream, struggling up through layers of heavy air. Her mind broke free.

Abruptly, the wendigo changed direction. The horizon blurred, and almost instantly they were flying over a forest of spruce trees, approaching the shore of Lake of the Woods. The Keewatin rose above the water, its windows burning with light. Below, Marla saw a clearing in the trees, and the little frame cabin. The wendigo fell toward the earth.

The ground rose up at her fast, in a disorienting rush. The wendigo landed hard. Marla screamed, and felt herself tumbling through the air.

Inside the cabin Tyrone felt the monster's hairy hand close around his arm. He was yanked off his feet, and the wendigo opened its huge mouth, exposing rows of tiny serrated teeth, cracked, broken, and yellow. A horrible stench spread through the room. Tyrone had no doubts that this was the wendigo White Eagle had warned them of, the one that had for centuries haunted the land where the Keewatin was built.

Tyrone's free arm still gripped the ax. He mustered all his strength and swung hard. The wendigo deflected it easily with its claw, ripping it from Tyrone's hand and flinging it aside. With a roar it hoisted Tyrone closer, exposing his throat and bending his arm to the breaking point.

Suddenly, the ceiling exploded. Shattered wood rained into the cabin. Marla's wendigo sprang from the starry night sky onto the one holding Tyrone, screaming in a long single tone like chalk screeching on a blackboard. Tyrone felt himself thrown aside. He hit the wall, immense pain racking his leg. The bone snapped.

Above him, the two great beasts were changing shape again, each of them growing bigger, swelling and rising until their antlers scraped the broken ceiling. The wendigos fell at each other, claws clutching at throat and eye, teeth imbedded in fur.

Tyrone twisted onto his stomach. He pulled himself across the doorstep to the porch and tumbled head-first down the steps. The pain in his leg was excruciating. He was covered with kerosene from the puddles on the floor. As soon as he lit a match, he'd turn into a human torch and set the rest of the cabin on fire. He dug his hand into his pocket, closed his fingers around the wooden matches.

"Tyrone!"

Marla stood five feet away. Wearing blue jeans and a sweatshirt, she was wet and covered with leaves and bits of bark. Her cheeks were red from the air of the altitudes.

Tyrone's face twisted with pain and his leg lay at an odd angle. Marla crouched beside him. He thrust the matches into her hand.

"Burn it! I doused it with gas!" His frantic plea was barely audible over the deafening bellows of the battling beasts. He pointed to the porch, where kerosene glistened on the floorboards. The cabin's roof exploded again. The wendigos were still changing, each one growing to equal the other's size. Marla's wendigo had the Keewatin's wendigo wrapped in a mortal embrace. With their antlers locked together, Marla's wendigo forced its opponent's head back and sank its teeth deep into its throat. The Keewatin wendigo's death groan rent the night air, anguished and shrill.

"Hurry!" Tyrone yelled. "It's the only way!"

Marla took the matches, struck one against a stone, and threw it onto the porch.

With a muffled blast, fire burst out in all directions, instantaneously following the trail of kerosene. The flames jumped into the air, crawling in the back door, igniting curtains, carpets, the wooden frames and moldings, climbing up through the jagged hole in the cabin's roof, leaping onto the fur of the struggling wendigos.

Marla's wendigo screamed as its fur caught fire. It flailed violently, smashing into wood and hurling pieces of the roof far into the air. Heat from the flames began to melt its icy skeleton. It shrank, collapsing like an empty bag.

A moan of inexhaustible yearning wrenched Marla's heart. The dying wendigo's mind reached out. Once again she saw cities of spiraling light and enchanted continents.

Save me. It called her.

She began to rise toward the fire.

I need you. Its voice was weakening, almost pathetic.

Marla came up hard against the beast's enormous longing. She refused to hear it anymore, refused to allow it even an inch of her own unhappiness, this creature that fed on sorrow. For all that the wendigo offered her, an existence beyond human with vistas of great beauty, she saw a trap, a ravenous hunger that could never be satisfied. And a heart that was frozen could never love, or be loved.

The flames consuming the cabin burned higher, reaching for the branches of the pine trees. The wendigo's frozen heart began to melt. It sank beneath the flames, its high-pitched screams growing thinner and weaker, until finally they ended. Only the crackle of the burning cabin sounded in the silent forest.

Marla huddled beside Tyrone, the heat from the fire warming them. Gradually, she became aware of distant sirens, shouts, activity behind them. People were rushing from the Keewatin toward the burning cabin.

She thought of the beauty the wendigo had showed her. She would keep those memories to herself. *No one needs to know how close I came,* Marla thought. It was like a whisper in her mind, a secret she would share only with the northern stillness, the pinpoint stars overhead, the icy wind stirring in the upper reaches of heaven. It was hers, and hers alone. And for the first time, she realized she had a life of her own.

"You okay?" Tyrone was looking at her. He forced a weak smile despite the pain in his broken leg.

"You saved my life," Marla told him.

Tyrone looked surprised. "I thought you saved mine."

Their eyes met and held for a second. Tyrone put his arms around Marla and pulled her closer. Her heart was pounding, warm, full of blood. She sank against him, her head falling against his chest. She held him tightly, glad that he was there.

ABOUT THE AUTHOR

ROBIN HARDY grew up in Canada. The setting of *The Call of the Wendigo* is the landscape of his childhood around the Canadian Shield. Mr. Hardy is the author of many popular books for young adults and divides his time between Tucson, Arizona, and New York City.

Read at your own risk. You may be
SCARED TO DEATH

Who is Bobby Wimmer stalking and why?

Enjoy the trio of SCARED TO DEATH thrillers:

- [ ] 0-553-56089-1 **BOBBY'S WATCHING;**
  Scared to Death #1 $3.50/$3.99 Can.

- [ ] 0-553-56096-4 **BOBBY'S BACK;**
  Scared to Death #2 $3.50/$3.99 Can.

- [ ] 0-553-56097-2 **BRIDESMAIDS IN BLACK;**
  Scared to Death #3 $3.50/$3.99 Can.

Buy them at your local bookstore or use this page for ordering.

Bantam Doubleday Dell
Books for Young Readers
2451 S. Wolf Road, Des Plaines, IL 60018

Please send me the items I have checked above. I am enclosing $_____ (Please add $2.50 to cover postage and handling). Send check or money order, no cash or C.O.D.s please.

MR./MS._____

ADDRESS_____

CITY/STATE_____ ZIP_____

Please allow four to six weeks for delivery.
Prices and availability subject to change without notice.   BFYR9-9/93

SPINE-TINGLING, BONE CHILLING STORIES

MIDNIGHT PLACE BOOKS BY SIMON LAKE

☐	0-553-29442-3	**DAUGHTER OF DARKNESS:** Midnight Place #1	$3.50/$3.99 Can.
☐	0-553-29791-0	**SOMETHING'S WATCHING:** Midnight Place #2	$3.50/$3.99 Can.
☐	0-553-56102-2	**DEATH CYCLE:** Midnight Place #3	$3.50/$3.99 Can.
☐	0-553-56168-5	**HE TOLD ME TO:** Midnight Place #4	$3.50/$3.99 Can.

BOOKS BY JOSEPH LOCKE

☐	0-553-29058-4	**KILL THE TEACHER'S PET**	$2.99/$3.50 Can.
☐	0-553-29653-1	**KISS OF DEATH**	$3.50/$3.99 Can.
☐	0-553-29657-4	**PETRIFIED**	$3.50/$3.99 Can.

Bantam Doubleday Dell Books for Young Readers
2451 South Wolf Road
Des Plaines, IL 60018

Please send the items I have checked above. I am enclosing $_____ (please add $2.50 to cover postage and handling). Send check or money order, no cash or C.O.D.s please.

NAME _____

ADDRESS _____

CITY _____ STATE _____ ZIP _____

Please allow four to six weeks for delivery.
Prices and availability subject to change without notice.

BFYR4-7/93